Tribal Melodies of Himachal Pradesh : Lahaul Valley

Tribal Melodies of Himachal Pradesh : Lahaul Valley

DR. MANORMA SHARMA

A.P.H. PUBLISHING CORPORATION

5, Ansari Road, Darya Ganj
New Delhi-110002

Published by

S.B. Nangia
A.P.H. Publishing Corporation
5, Ansari Road, Darya Ganj
New Delhi-110002
☎ 3274050

ISBN 81-7024-942-2

1998

Typesetting at
NEW APCON
25/2, Panchsheel Shopping Centre
New Delhi 110 017
☎ 6490802

Printed in India at
Efficient Offset Printers
New Delhi-110035

CONTENTS

PROLOGUE

In a country like India, which is multilingual, diverse in characters and where peasantry constitutes the largest segment of population, knowledge of folk institutions, their habits, customs, traditions and culture serve as significant tools in the process of motivating the rural masses towards development. They prove a useful means for the upliftment of the common people and national reconstruction. Folklore traditions could help reinforce the sense of national identity, socio-economic development and social progress more easier and acceptable to rural masses.

Folklore studies form an essential part in any scheme of study dealing with the evolution of people's social, emotional and cultural life, and is also an index to their ethical, aesthetic norms and sense of values. A study of the folklore reveals people's ideas and ideals, hopes and fears, aspirations and superstitions. India is a land full of folklores with its age-old civilization, rich cultural heritage, myths, legends, folk verses and a rich legacy which has been handed down from generation to generation. The study of folklore is a reliable and a trustworthy index to know the background of the people as it fostered cultural unity and national integration despite its diverse languages, religions, regions and times.

There has been an easy mobility of folklore through pilgrimages, fairs, festivals and rituals. The wandering minstrels, saints (sadhus) and fakirs have also played an important role in disseminating them throughout the length and breadth of this country. People of the north visiting the temples of the South and vice-versa carry their folk tales, songs, riddles, and proverbs with them and there is inconspicuous integration. The "Dharamsalas", inns, and choltries, where the pilgrims rest and intermingle are the places which work as the clearing houses of information for the folk tales, traditional songs and riddles. Thus, we find a common pattern in folk-literature of different regions from Kashmir to Kanya Kumari, of course, with slight regional variations. They were handed over from one generation to other generation through oral tradition before they came to be reproduced to writing and constituted the cultural background of the country and its people.

Folklore is such an aspect of culture which explains people's socio-cultural systems, beliefs, values and attitudes through folk-songs, folk-dances, folk-tales, proverbs, riddles, legends, ballads, fables, charms, fairs, festivals, religions, superstitions, customs and traditions. The field of folklore is extensive and provides a rich treasure of human experiences. It is the oral tradition of the people which is transmitted through the process of socialization.

The study of various aspects of folklore may eventually solve many difficult problems of national unity and national character. This type of study portrays contemporary life, documents traditional behaviour, reinforces systems of belief, and provides safety-valves to release pent up resentments. It throws light on the numerous aspects, of a social organisation and provides clues to an understanding of the interplay between culture and personality development. The study of folklore can also help in understanding acculturation, patterns of the relation between culture and environment, as also between culture and personality. India is a land steeped in folklore, with its ancient civilization, rich cultural heritage, myths, legends, folk-lores and the like. Only a few countries in the world could come to the level of Indian folklore in their richness, depth and wisdom. All literature, oral or written — springs from life, but oral literature is a better projection of the innermost recesses of the socio-cultural life of a society and its traditions, customs, social values, rites and rituals. It is a matter of great concern that folk culture is dying under the forces of development, urbanization and modernization. Moreover, the technological development and revolution in electronics have contributed much in corrupting the folklore culture. Thus, there is a great need to preserve, document and protect our rich cultural heritage and to spread awareness about the folklore treasure. To get fully acquainted with the essence of folklore, the different areas of folklore studies must be explored. Folklore consists of folk literature and folk-music as the two major components. Folk stories, folk tales, proverbs, riddles are part of folk literature, whereas folk music consists of folk songs, folk dance, folk drama and musical instruments accompanying them.

It is really surprising that the "Wonderland of Himachal Pradesh Lahaul", has been a neglected area as for as the study of folk music is concerned. The area has diverse cultural history due to intermixing of cultural milieus of the adjoining areas. Thus the difference in language, art, culture and music is clearly evident from the life-style of people of Lahaul which is a tribal area of Himachal Pradesh and this tribe is popularly known as "Lahaula". Keeping in view the importance of folk music, the author has tried to collect various facets of folk music and has notated them by following the traditional style of Indian musical notation system.

The accent, diction and pronunciation of the local language is quite different and it is desirable that the proper pronunciation is followed. It is quite difficult to write the dialectical words in "Roman" yet effort has been made to write them to their nearest pronunciation.

The author is highly thankful to the people of Lahaul who have helped in collecting the desired data. Special thanks are due to Sh. Chhep Ram Dogra who rendered the folk songs which he got from his father, unfortunately, who is no more now. But it is a matter of great satisfaction that the rich folk tradition has now been preserved in black and white which he had received from his father. Thanks are also due to Himachal Pradesh Tourism Development Corporation, the Directorate of Public Relations, Himachal Pradesh and the Census Department, Government of India for providing easy access to the literature.

I am greatly indebted to Sh. Rai, Hon'ble State Minister for Tribal Development, H.P. Government, Shimla for extending very useful information through discussion and providing some rare photographs about the culture of Lahaulas.

Shimla   **Dr. Manorma Sharma**

Chapter I
LAHAUL - LAND

The present district of Lahaul and Spiti are two distinct entities—geographically and historically. Sandwiched between Kullu in the south and Ladakh and Zanskar in the north lies the predominantly Buddhist region of Lahaul and Spiti. The Sutlej river divides the region into many ranges and high valleys. Lahaul area includes valleys of the Chandra and Bhaga rivers up to their junction near Tandi and also the main Chandra Bhaga valley as far as Thirot Nallah which also is called Chamba Lahaul. Spiti area includes the valley of the main Spiti river and the valley of its tributary the Pin river. The valleys of Spiti and Lahaul remain almost cut off from each other for 8 months of the year by its mighty wall of Himalayan ranges between them. It is only through Kunzum La Pass with its 15,000 ft height which permits the passage in the remaining 4 months from July to October.

According to J.Hutchinson and Vogel the first historical mention of Lahaul is found in Hiuen Tsang travelogue who visited Kullu somewhere between 629-645 AD. He mentioned Lo-u-lo (Lahaul) as lying north of Kiu-lu-to (Kullu).

Incidentally, the name Lahaul had been in use in whole of the world except the local population and the Tibetans call this area as Garzha.

It is believed that Lahaul in the ancient times had been ruled by the local chieftains called Jos which corresponded to the Ranas and the Thakurs of the rest of the hill states. These *Jos* were believed to be of Tibetan origin and the only symbol of their subjection of the people was the annual tribute which they used to pay to Jos. These Baronial families mainly were said to be living at Ghushal, Kardang, Darcha, Barbog and some other places like the *Jagirdar* or Thakur families during the British time. From about 600 AD onwards until the first half of the 19th century Lahaul was an intermittent battle-ground between the kings of Kullu, Chamba, Ladakh and the Tibet. From the ups and downs of the battle and the consequent territorial adjustments, it would appear that the valley beyond Tandi to Thirot Nallah was largely under the occupation of the king of Chamba during this period and the area from the *Sangam* (junction) of Chandra and Bhaga rivers upto Kunzum and the Bhaga valley upto Baralacha Pass had been under the Kullu king. In between, it appears particularly the Bhaga valley had been under the domain of the Ladakh king. It is also indicated that hordes of invaders from Central Asia (Yarkand) invaded the entire Chandra and Bhaga valleys and they reached as far as Brahmpura (Bharmaur) in Chamba. Whatever be the state of actual occupation it is, however, true that the Lahaul valley remained under the Central Asian invaders for a considerable period of time as the cultural and ethnic impacts left by them are visible even today.

PHYSICAL FEATURES

The Lahaul and Spiti district has an area of 13,688 sq. km. It is bounded between Thirot Nallah in the west to Samdu in the east, Baralacha Pass and its parallel ranges in the north to the Bhabha, Parvati, Hamta, Rohtang and Kugti and the Sach pass in the south. It touches the Tibet on its eastern border and north to it lies the Ladakh, on the western and southern side it borders with Chamba and Kullu districts of Himachal Pradesh. On the south-eastern side is the Kinnaur district. The precise location of the district is between north latitude 31° 44' 47" and 32° 59' 57" and between east longitude 76° 46' 29" and 78° 41' 34".

The Lahaul and Spiti valleys differ from each other in their physical features to some extent: Spiti valley is broad, enchanting and completely rugged without any green vegetation worth the name, while the Lahaul valley is narrow and steep but studded with green patches of poplar, willow and other coniferous forests. The Spiti valley has minimum altitude of about 3000 m at the entrance to 5000 m near Kunzum La. The Lahaul valley has lower elevation, broadly ranging between about 2100 m at the exit (Thirot Nallah) to about 4600 m near the source of the Chandra and the Bhaga rivers. But both the valleys have very high rugged mountains covered with massive snow and glaciers rising as high as 6400 m above sea level.

Both the valleys are, indeed, star studded with enormous rivers and rivulets. The main amongst the numerous rivers in Lahaul are: the Chandra river which originates from the Chandra Tal near the Baralacha and it extends downwards up to the Tandi, the other river is the Bhaga which originates from the Suraj Tal opposite the Baralacha and meets the Chandra river at the Tandi and beyond Tandi the two rivers amalgamate into the Chandra Bhaga or the Chenab river adding numerous foaming, fretting and splashing rivulets on the way until they leave the district at the Thirot Nallah to the Pangi and onwards to Pakistan and ultimately immortalises itself into Arabian Sea.

In the Spiti valley, the main river is the Spiti river which originates from the heights of the Kunzum La and swallows on its way numerous rivers and rivulets. The other famous river joining it is the Pin river which has its source near the Bhabha Pass and ultimately joins the Spiti river from the right side. From the left side the rivers that join the Spiti river are the Lingti, the Gumto and the Parechu.

Closely associated with the high elevation and snow mountain ranges, are the glaciers and icecaves in the district, the famous being known as the Bara Shigri or the big glacier. Captain Harcourt who visited this glacier in 1869 puts its width as nearly two miles. Across this Bara Shigri is another glacier known as the Chhota Shigri. Other famous glaciers are the Gangstang near the border of the Lahaul region, the Sanapani glacier which also is visible from the Rohtang Pass and the Perad glacier, a small but accessible which has a ice-cave in which cuttings of various species are being raised. Community plantation is also being emphasized which is subsidized by the Government up to 50 per cent on fencing and plantation etc.

Lahaul is marked by a central mass of almost uniformly high mountains and massive glaciers. The two rivers, the Chandra and the Bhaga which rise on either side of the Bara Lacha Pass flow through the narrow valleys. Lahaul is also a fascinating area for the Buddhist art and culture. The monasteries of the Lahaul and the Spiti are rich repositories of ancient murals, *Thankas*, wood carving and golden images of the Padma-Sambhava. The people are charming, friendly and hospitable with their own traditional dances, ballads, folk tales and legends.

The sole access to Lahaul is the 3,915 m high Rohtang Pass which according to a legend was formed when the mythical Tibetan king Gyepo Gyesar hit the mountains with his magical hunting whip, to make a way to the Kullu valley. Another legend says that when the people of Lahaul approached the Hindu God Shiva, to create a path across the mountains so that they could visit the land of Kullu, the lord hit the mountains thus creating the pass. The narration is as follows:—

"Lord Shiva took his whip and smote the mountains, again and again. There was a rushing and a terrible crushing and storms and winds so strong that mountains swayed before them and many rocks fell from the mountains.

Then there was a great silence over the land, and with it a great darkness. For everything even the *Nallahs* and the sun and the birds stopped and stood still before the majesty of Lord Shiva."

PHYSICAL REGIONS

The most conspicuous characteristics of this valley are the high pinnacled mountains and narrow river valleys which divides the valley into different sub-valleys.

i)   Chandra valley called Rangloi.

ii) Bhaga Valley

iii) Pattan Valley

iv) Lingti maidan

v)   The main valley

(I) The Chandra Valley

This begins from the snow bed on the south-eastern foot of the Baralacha Pass. For the first 72 km the valley is barren and uninhabited, with high peaks and large glaciers tapering downwards from snow-fields on the tops of ridges. The slopes are characteristically stony and bare. Pastures exist in patches only along the valley where the *Gaddis* camp during the summer season.

The Rangloi contains four *Kothis* of Khoksar, Sissu, Gondhla and Ghushal. Khoksar is the first village in the valley. From there on scenery becomes greener and less oppressive. The valley on the right bank broadens out, villages are more frequent and cultivated areas are more through the middle of the valley. On the left is a sheer mountain wall from the river bed to the rugged crest. Beyond Gondhla, however, the topography to the left also becomes less rugged and the mountain slopes are gentle, with terraced fields sloping down to the river.

(II) The Bhaga Valley

This valley starts from the south-western foot of Baralacha Pass. It is also barren, rocky and uninhabited up to Darcha which is the first village in this valley. It is situated at the junction of Yoche *Nallah* and the Zangskarcha with the main river. From here the valley broadens and the right bank has large tracts of level and cultivable land. Almost after every 7 or 8 km there is a village.

From Darcha to Kolong, the valley is called Stod and from Kolong to Keylong it is called Gaar. Keylong is the largest village or town of Lahaul which is on the right bank of river Bhaga and it is the headquarters of the district. There are precipitous cliffs on the left bank but in the lower part, the slopes become gentler and there are some villages on the left bank also.

Kardang, the one time capital of Lahaul and the seat of a famous monastery, lies on a commanding spot opposite Keylong. Gaar contains four Kothis—Kardang, Barbog, Kolong and Gungrang.

(III) The Pattan Valley

It is a combined valley of the rivers, the Chandra and the Bhaga which starts from the Tandi where the Chandra and the Bhaga rivers meet and ends at Thirot on the boundary with Chamba district. It is a broader, more fertile and thickly populated valley. This valley has six Kothis — Tandi, Warpa, Ranika, Shansha, Jalma and Jobrang.

(IV) The Lingti Maidan

Across the Baralacha Pass, towards the north is a vast tract of land about 260 sq km in area which is almost uncultivated and uninhabited, the lowest elevation is 4270 m. The plains are pastures which are used for grazing animals by the *Gaddis* during the summer season.

The plain is dissected by the Lingti river which meets the Yunan river and the combined stream then runs north-east to meet the Tsarab river before flowing north into the Zanskar.

(V) The Main Valley

A great triangle is formed between the two streams of the Chandra and the Bhaga rivers, which forms the centre of the area. From outside, this great mass of mountains presents the spectacle of a huge fort with more or less evenly scattered settlements. Here and there, the sheer wall is broken forming a deep furrow, revealing on the top a huge tapering glacier and a torrential *Nallah* gushing forth from underneath it. The highest of these is the Samundari glacier with two branches, each 16 km long with a spout about 3 km wide opening into the Chandra river. The main axis of the central mass lies from north to south with a branch going west towards the Tandi. On the top of the mass are lateral spurs with interesting valleys filled with glaciers and perpetual snow. The peaks rise to over 6400 m above sea level and include the Gyephang Peak which can be seen from Shimla.

The Bhaga river flows at some distance from the northern and western heights, and numerous torrents pour into it from the glaciers placed in the angle formed by these mountains, as well as a large stream which joins the left bank from the central mass. The Baralacha Pass is an important feature in the general configuration of the region. It is nearly 8 km long and consists of a high neck of land connecting the central mountains with the main Himalaya. Its name implies "Pass with cross roads on summit", roads from Zangskar, Ladakh, Spiti and Lahaul meet at the top. The pass gives off on the north-west and the Bhaga river on the north, the Yunan river on the south-west belonging to the central hill and thus passes between the sources of the other two rivers.

This valley is further sub-divided into four distinct parts:-

a. Changsa valley

b. Loksa valley

c. Gahari valley

d. Totapa valley

a. Changsa Valley. The part of Lahaul which is spread between Tindi and the boundary of Lahaul from its neighbouring area is known as Changsa valley. It is also called Pattan valley.

b. Loksa Valley. The area from Tandi and the whole valley of Chandra till Khoksar is the territory of Loksa valley.

c. Gahari Valley. The area which is situated on both the sides of the river Bhaga near Keylong is called Gahari valley.

d. Totapa Valley. The area beyond Keylong till the boundary of Lahaul valley is known as Totapa valley or Tot valley.

ARCHAEOLOGICAL IMPORTANCE

Following monuments of Lahaul depict the culture, religion, customs and history of the region since no written evidence of past are available:-

1. Kardang Gompa
2. Trilok Nath Temple
3. Mirkula Temple

1. Kardang Gompa

It is believed that Kardang Gompa was built by the Lama Rimpo. There are four chapels in this Gompa. In one of these chapels there are the ashes of Lama Rimpoch. The walls of this Gompa are beautifully painted. There are idols made of brass. These are called *Kundre* in the local language. Along the second wall there are pious scriptures written in the Bhoti language. In one of the rooms there are musical instruments and costumes which are worn for the "Mask Dance".

2. Trilok Nath Temple

The idol of Trilok Nath Temple is made of ivory. People believe that this is the idol of Lord Shiva but some believe that it is of Lord Buddha. According to a legend, a shepherd brought this idol to the place where it is installed. People also believe that when the shepherd brought this from the Hindsa village, it used to speak and on the direction of the idol it was installed in Trilok

Nath Temple.

3. Mirkula Temple

The idol of Mirkula Temple is made of the mixed metals. The paintings on the walls of the temple are different from other temples of the region and there is a great similarity in the style of painting which is like the Deccan School. The whole of the paintings which are done on the walls are on the wood of a single tree. There are two wooden structures on the both sides of the main door of the temple. These are the security guards which are known as *Bhairon* in local dialect. It seems that these soldiers are ready to go to the battle-field holding the swords in their hands.

PLACES OF HISTORICAL, ARCHAEOLOGICAL AND TOURIST IMPORTANCE

In Lahaul, the monasteries combine archaeological and historical significance. Amongst them the most important is the Kardang monastery opposite Keylong on the left side of the Bhaga river in the Bhaga valley and the other is Triloknath temple in Pattan Valley. All these monasteries date their history as old as between 600 AD to 800 AD. The Kardang monastery has its origin during the days of Padma Sambhava of Udyana who propagated the Buddhism in the valley. The Triloknath temple traces its history even earlier to that when it was a Hindu temple and even today it continues to be a holy place for both Hindus and Buddhists. The murals on the walls of Kardang monastery are matchless in their finish. Guru Ghantal Monastery in the Chandra valley is also associated with Padma Sambhava, the Buddhist missionary of the 8th century. There are the idols of Buddha, Brijeshwari Devi etc.

These monasteries are also the greatest centres of the tourist attraction and every year thousands of people visit for prayers to these monasteries. Lahaul and Spiti district is not suitable for tourists who prefer easy life and luxury living. It is, of course, a place of great interest and inspiration to those who have spirit of adventure and faculty for its admiration to appreciate the difficult geophysical features, with its massive snow covered mountains pinnacling deep into the sky and massive glaciers and ice caves in innumerable depressions of mountain ranges. The steep gorges of the Bhaga and the Chandra rivers and the broad flat rugged valley have an immense joy to give. The Chandra Tal and the Suraj Tal with their spotless white swans swimming in the ice cold waters put the visitors to ecstasy. Most of the tourists do not venture to see these places. Keylong Tourist Bungalow is usually occupied by the foreign visitors and rarely a native visitor reaches there. Bulk of the tourists are content with going up to Rohtang Pass alone and be safe back at Manali.

Keylong

A village amidst green fields of barley and buck-wheat, Keylong is the headquarters of the Lahaul and Spiti district. It is 117 km from Manali by a motorable road. Keylong is like a barbaric jewel, a roughly cut emerald in bronze and silver setting. An oasis of green fields and willow trees planted along the water courses is surrounded by brown hills and snowy heights. There are a number of Buddhist monasteries within easy reach of the town. The old Kharding (Keylong) Lahaul is a wonderland since it has attraction for all categories of people right from the rural to the highly professional and experts. One can enjoy all sorts of natural scenic beauty of valleys, rivers, glaciers, pastures, forts, *gompas*, monasteries and temples. People live in small villages which have scattered houses. The area is sparsely populated due to steep terrains and high mountains and lack of plain area but people are industrious and not professional or businessmen. Following are some of the places of interest from cultural, historical and tourism point of view. This is the only village in Lahaul that has a planned market which caters to the needs of inhabitants.

Tandi

It is a legendary village with mythological personages. Rivers Chandra and Bhaga unite here into an eternal wedlock. Tandi is 102 km from Manali and 6 km away from Keylong. It is believed that it was founded by Raja Rana Chand who christened this as Chandi but with time it changed to Tandi.

Triloknath Temple

This is an important place of pilgrimage in the Pattan valley. Triloknath idol is a six armed image of white marble of Avalokiteshvara, Bodhisatva. Some believe it to be of lord Shiva and the legend about the establishment of this temple is described in one of the folk song is the next chapter. Visitors enjoy crossing the Chandra-Bhaga rivers and the trek of 3 km to reach destination.

This shrine houses a six armed statue seated in the lotus position and carved in white marble. Two hands are placed in the posture of meditation, one holds a lotus, two rest over the chest in praying position and the last bestows gifts. This temple has fascinating legends and is example of fine stone carving. People have great faith in the blessings from this temple.

In the village of Udaypur, is an ancient temple dedicated to the goddess *Durga* deplicted as *Mahishasurmardini* and this image is of eight metals *(Ashtadhatu)*. Panels on the interiors have paintings from the episodes of Mahabharata and Ramayana.

Mirkula Temple

The Buddhists regard this as temple of Mirkula i.e.*Marici Vajravarahi*. Udaypur is 166 km from Manali.

Batal

From here one can trek to the Chandra Tal and also go up to Bara- lacha Pass, on the Manali-Leh Road.

Bara Shigri Glacier

Situated on the left bank of the Chandra River, the mouth of this long glacier is 4 km from Batal.

Kaksar/Kboksar

21 km beyond Rohtang Pass situated at the height of 3140 m is the coldest place in Lahaul which is a shelter place for trekkers. It is the highest village of the Chandra valley. Buddhist pilgrimage is important. *Lama* has control over the village.

Gondhla

It is a village of royal houses which is 18 km from Keylong on the right bank of river Chandra. Village Gompa is of historical importance and of tourist attraction.

MONASTERIES

There are 18 monasteries in Lahaul and each one has a special significance. Some of these are:-

1. Kardang Monastery

It is visible from the Keylong village and is situated across the Bhaga river and is about 5 km from Keylong. It is one of the biggest but latest monastery in this region which was probably built in 12th century but was rebuilt by Norbu Lama in the beginning of the current century.

2. Shashur Monastery

This is situated on a hillock about 3 km from Keylong towards north. The monastery is built on a rectangular block which is plastered over by mud and white-washed. It has a flat roof decorated with typical Buddhist flags. The second store of the building has valuable paintings representing the brief history of the 84 Buddhas. Fair in June-July is held every year. Mask dance is performed by Lama and other followers.

3. Tayal Monastery or Gompa

It is 6 km from Keylong and is one of the oldest monasteries of the Lahaul valley and has a long (5m) statue of Guru Padma Sambhava alongwith a library.

4. Guru Ghantal Monastery

On the right bank of the river Chandra at a distance of 4 km from the Tandi is situated this monastery which is associated with *Padmasambhava* of 8th century. The monastery has the idols of Buddha, *Brajeshwari Devi* and others. A festival, Ghantal is held every year on 15th Lunar day of *Ashadh* month (mid June). On this day, the visitors or pilgrims have a round of the sacred mountain which is about 29 km and they go on foot since the path is not even.

Baralacha pass

About 75 km from Keylong on the Manali-Leh road, there is Baralacha Pass which is at the height of about 4883 m above sea level and is about 8 km long. Roads from Zangskar, Ladakh, Spiti and Lahaul meet on the top of it.

LAKES

Among the lakes two famous lakes — the Chandra Tal and the Suraj Tal are situated at such an height which is beyond the imagination of a common tourist or visitor. The Chandra Tal is about 6 km from Kunzam Pass while the other lake, the Suraj Tal from which the Bhaga river originates is situated below the summit of the Baralacha Pass. According to another legend, it is believed that Tandi word originated from Tan-dehi i.e. leaving the body. It is said that *Draupadi*, the wife of the *Pandavas* had left her body here for going to heavenly abode. Still another legendary belief is that the dead body of *Vasishatha* was cremated at this place. Thus, it can be assumed that this is one of the oldest village which might have some association with the life of the Pandavas.

CLIMATE AND RELATED INFORMATION

The climate in the district is quite variable, the temperature goes below minus 20 degree Celsius during winter and 26 degree in summer and as such it is temperate. The winter season is from the mid of November to March and is followed by spring which lasts for a month or so and is then followed by summer of 4 months and finally there is autumn for 6 weeks in October-November.

Summers in the valley are cool and pleasant with green grass and alpine flowers and variety of crops. There is no monsoon in Lahaul and this enables climbers and trekkers to enjoy a long and unbroken season in perpetual sunshine and dry crisp air of Lahaul and explore the wilderness and grandeur of the inner Himalayas. Here the Himalayas present a different sight, brown barren slopes and icy rivers and streams that gush around rocks and boulders after emerging from giant glaciers. In these mountains there are the passes that lead to Leh, peaks that challenge mountaineers, a varied wildlife that attracts nature lovers and a terrain that is a hikers delight. In these heights are hidden scenic spots like the Chandra Tal, the Suraj Tal and the valleys of the Chandra and Bhaga rivers that later becomes the Chenab on entering the Kashmir Valley.

CHAPTER - II
THE PEOPLE

The people of Lahaul are a mix race. According to J. Hutchinson and Vogel, the linguistics research indicates that in remote time about 2000 BC, the area was inhabited by an aborigine tribe who in language and also perhaps in stock, were analogous to the *Munda* speaking tribe of Bengal and central India. It is believed that this tribe must have borrowed words from the vocabulary of their Tibetan neighbourers on north-east and east who must have constantly come in contact with them as nomadic traders or invaders. Even till the beginning of 20th century Hutchison and Vogel maintained that the survivors of the *Munda* speaking ethnological stock were found in the isolated village of Malana in Kullu and in the Bushair track on the Sutlej. At later period Tibetan settlers came into the head of Bhaga valley and from Spiti and Tibet into head of Chandra valley. Aryans and semi-Aryans also came from west and south in the valley on the different stocks and started living. Thus, the Lahaulas at present are the ultimate product of the amalgamation of these different races. Unlike the Lahaul Valley, the Spitians are purely the Tibetan stock and any traces of Hindu or Aryan blood in the Spiti valley is not seen today. On the other hand, even the features of the Lahaulas of today show a combination of Mangolian and Aryan traits with their short and stout physique, slightly high cheek bones and oblique almond shaped eyes combined with straight noses.

The Lahaulas being of ancient times, lived in far flung areas in forests and other inaccessible valleys and so remained cut off from the rest of the world and were not exposed to the modern technology and happenings and thus, they had faith in old or primitive beliefs. Their sense of aloofness in immense solitude gave rise to certain "psychological pride positions" toward the adoption of supernatural solutions for the problems of existence. Thus, they started to believe in spirits, ghosts, devils, etc. and this led to the practice of sacrifice. The modern Lahuala men are very active and shrewd and widely travelled to Tibet, Ladakh, Kullu, Punjab and Calcutta and have a considerable business acumen.

Because of their perhaps ethnographic cross breeding, people are short, sturdy and very hardworking. Before the start of modern communtcation system the male folks mainly spent their time by trading on their mules apart from helping the ladies in agricultural operations and later men shuttled from Tibet to Punjab and Calcutta, women attended the uneconomical agricultural operations like sowing, irrigation of barley and buck-wheat. But now with the opening of the modern communication system, the men folk are seen carrying their trade in trucks which have replaced the mules and the women folk work on the field mainly concentrating on cash crops like seed potatoes which has, indeed revolutionized the economy of the valley.

DRESS

During winter (about 8 months) men wear woollen coat and woollen *pyjamas* and women wear tight pyjamas. Both are of thick woollen cloth which is mostly spun and wooven by them during winters. Colours are mostly dark. *Choga* like shirts are tightened at the waist with the waist coat. Most of the times women wear clothes of red, maroon, crimson and dark brown colour. Mostly the men's robes are buttoned on the right and women robes have strings in front in place of buttons. The robe is secured at the waist with a sash. Women always wear green or yellow jacket over the robe. During summer, men wear cotton clothes while women wear *Shaneel* clothes. Men wear cap that resemble the Kullu cap while ladies wear round disclike caps. In general, unmarried girls do not wear any head dress. Bodh ladies remain bare headed. Men keep short hair while women keep their hair twisted into numerous pigtails held in position by plaites.

Lahulas have traditional jute shoes, the soles of which are made of barley straw and the upper part is beautifully embroidered with multicoloured wool. This type of foot-wear is used inside the house while all other types of footwear are seen outside the house. No one is without a footwear outside the house. They put on the shoes etc. as suited to their local needs and conditions. These shoes are very suitable for walking on the snow. The traditional shoes also are indicative of the social status, as well-to-do classes wear shoes which are furlined.

ORNAMENTS

Lahauli women folk are fond of wearing different types of ornaments and these ornaments are mostly of gold. These are profusely studded with beads which may be of red, green or blue in colour. They worship the ornaments before wearing. Following are the most common ornaments worn by men and women:-

Along

These are ear-rings of gold or brass that are studded with white or coloured beads, whether original or imitation. They may weigh about 15-25 g. These are worn by women of all ages and castes.

Bada Phull

It is a gold nose pin or plug worn by married women but not by a widow. These are also embedded with beads.

Chhota Phulli

It is a nose pin which is smaller in size than the Bara Phull. It is also of gold and weighs about 5 g and is worn by women of all ages except widows.

Dangkri

A square shaped piece of silver or shell is tied over the pigtail of women. It has small strings of beads which are used for tieing it with the tuft of hairs made in different shapes usually a straight plait is preferred. Sometimes small bells of brass are also tied at the ends of the strings.

Dunkertsa

This is an ornament used by Bodh women of all ages. It is made of silver with a bead in the centre and weighs about 200 g. This is worn at the back near the waist where all the ends of different plaits of hair are gathered. This is worn on festivities.

Guithah

It is a gold or silver ring embedded with beads which is worn by men and women.

Kirkitsi

It is a cup shaped ornament of silver having two clips at the bottom for tieing or fixing over the hair. It is worn by women of all ages, particularly the old ladies. Unmarried girls do not wear it. It is rarely of gold. Usually, it is worn on festive occasions but old women wear it for most part of the year.

Kyix Kyirts

A saucer shaped silver ornament is worn over the back of head on the plaits of hair. Usually many plaits are made and they are tied almost near the centre of back of head where this ornament is tied.

Murki

These are ear-rings which are simple in construction and are circular in shape. These are worn by male members only. It is a gold ornament which is common with men of all castes.

Mutig-kanti

This ornament is for the head of women of all ages and castes. White beads are knitted in threads with sets of corals. In the middle is a piece of gold which usually hangs down. It may also be studded with beads. Women wear it daily.

Nang

These are a pair of silver bangles which may be weighing upto 250 gm and are worn by women of all ages and castes.

Phans

These are silver ornaments. These are worn by women on either side of the head over the hair to hide the red threads (ties) used to tie the Poshel with the plait. Most of the women wear this ornament.

Poshel

It is a pair of round balls made of a substance known as *Kapur*. Every ball has a hole in which a small piece of gold or silver is fixed. Ball is worn/tied on either side of the forehead and is tied with the help of a red thread to the plait at the back of the head. This thread is covered by Phans.

Pholunu

It is a silver chain which is studded with imitation beads. The length may be 60-75 cm. It is an ornament usually worn by Bodh women. Different ends of Pholunu are again gathered and then attached to *Chabu* from which are hanging the different silver chains producing sound. There is a hook with which the Pholunu is twisted and attached with the *Cholu* (gown)

Shamsham

It is a collection of 5 to 7 chain like silver strands in which are embedded imitation beads. At the lower end of each string, there is a Chabu which produces sound. From the Chabu hang differently shaped small and thin silver pieces used separately for cleaning ears, teeth, nails etc. It is attached with Chabu in the front. This is worn by women folk.

Tarka

To keep the hair in position over the forehead, these clip like ornaments made of silver are used. It is also used by ladies of all ages. Usually two Tarkas are used, one on either side of forehead but more are also in use.

Tuk-kanti

It is a necklace which has beads of coral and the lower end has a special type of stone. Most of the women wear this chain.

Yutod

It is a round cap, the interior of which is made of thick cotton cloth over which is stitched red cotton cloth. Four pieces of golden ribbon (metalic) usually 12 mm wide and 75 mm long are stitched on to the red cloth. *Zari* work is done on this golden ribbon. The remaining space is embedded with turquoise. In the front there are, a silver moon and a sun joined together with short silver chains hanging down to produce sound. Beads may also be fixed over it. This portion hangs over the forehead when the cap is worn. It is worn by Bodh women.

SOCIAL MODES

People of Lahaul and Spiti have little inhibition. Boys and girls freely mix without any restraint and love marriages consequently are very common.

Though Lahaul valley traditionally had polyandry system, but, it is now on a steady decline. The law of primogeniture prevailed in both the valleys where the entire landed property was inherited by the eldest brother and others had to earn their livelihood by engaging themselves in service, trade and by becoming Lamas in the monasteries. This in the past acted as a double-edged sword by stabilising agricultural economy and also controlling population. The polyandry prevented fragmentation of the family land.

The social celebrations in both valleys follow with the feast which consists of meat and Chhang, the local brew.

As is well known, the entire population of Lahaul and Spiti district is tribal and of course, a meagre number being scheduled castes. There are three types of tribes in the district. They are

Swanglas and *Lahaulas* who are mostly in Lahaul Division and Bodh/Bodhs mostly in Spiti Division.

MARRIAGE

Social customs of Lahaul are quite different from other hill areas. The marriage custom is also quite different. There used to be polyandry in the past but now this custom has totally vanished. The young boys and girls do not like this custom.

Three types of marriages are being conducted in Lahaul.

1. Arranged marriage
2. Love marriage.
3. Marriage by force.

1. Arranged Marriage

This type of marriage is solemnised with the approval of the parents of the boy and girl and they arrange the marriage. Though ceremonies performed during the wedding are similar to the other hill areas but in Lahaul, the girl or boy does not go in the palanquin. There had been no tradition that the bride or bride-groom has to move in the palanquin for the wedding.

A local brewed drink called *Lugadi*, is served and the boys and girls dance vigorously thus, celebrating the marriage.

2. Love Marriage

This type of marriage is solemnised with the consent of the boy and girl who like each other and later they seek the approval of their respective parents. To get the approval, the boy's parents send wine and other gifts to the girl's parents. If the parents of the girl accept the gifts and wine, the marriage is solemnised which is mostly accepted as there is no inhibition. Since the boy and girl like each other, they may get married prior to the approval from their respective parents and thus afterwards the parents also reconcile and accept the girl as their daughter-in-law.

3. Marriage by Force

It is a very strange style of marriage. The boy forcibly takes away the girl of his choice with the help of his friends and the girl has to marry him against her will. Sometimes the boy only touches the girl and other people take the girl to the boy's house and compel the girl to marry that boy. The girl has to do against her wishes. Now-a-days, boys do not like this type of marriage but still the marriageable girls take every precaution while going out especially going from one village to other with the fear that some boy and his friend may not take her away forcibly.

POSITION OF WOMEN

The position of women in a tribe affects its social organization and its conception of marital rights and duties. The joint family system is predominant among the Bhot community which is primarily a consequence of polyandry and still persists in this region. In the polyandrous unions, the brothers live as co-husbands sharing one wife. The common wife also commands a responsible and respectable status in the family. The value of the wife lies principally in her services as a house-hold drudge. She produces children, cooks food, cuts grass, gathers wood, fetches water and does all the work in the field except actual ploughing. The marriage among Bhot is not a matter of affection or championship. It has mere economic connection. Because of this factor she enjoys the place of honour and respect in the family and as such she has control over the entire household affairs.

In polyandrous union, a wife sharing several brothers has to extend great adroitness, diplomacy and self-control to maintain the unity of the house. She has sexual as well as economic control to affect over each brother who at different stages in his development will have different needs. As the younger brother matures, she initiates him sexually and then accommodates him with the others.

Bhot marriage is remarkable in its simplicity. Consent of both the parties or of their guardians followed by the entry of the bride in the house of the man as wife, constitutes a valid marriage under the custom. No priest or public authority is needed to solemnize the marriage. The dissolution of the marriage is equally simple. On the basis of information, it appears that there are two critical periods in the development of a marriage during which divorce is most likely to occur. In each period the pattern of divorce is different. The first stage of instability occurs in the early years of marriage, generally before children are born. The second, which usually attacks polyandric units, develops when the role of the brothers sharing a common wife changes with the senior enjoying less prestige and the junior assuming more importance and confidence in the household.

In the first kind, morality of the wife or change of religion by her, entitles husband to seek divorce while a wife on account of impotency, leprosy, change of religion etc, are the grounds on which she can claim divorce. The divorce on the basis of one of the above grounds is sought at an early date after the marriage. Normally another wife is brought into the house with the consent of the first wife. After the lapse of more time and with the arrival of children in the family, marriage partners repose greater confidence in each other and chances of divorce are automatically reduced on such grounds.

Though with the lapse of time, a wife consolidates her position in the household, there may arise a situation where the elder brother may be forced to leave the house. Such a situation arises during a shift in economic and sexual roles among brothers in polyandry. When the younger man (husband) starts taking more responsibility, the wife may favour him and in doing so may neglect the elder husband. In such a situation, if he cannot adjust himself to his new status or the wife does not restore the balance, he may quit the house. When an elder brother leaves, the next brother assumes the leadership of the house with the wife. In such situations, generally the departing spouse is awarded a share of the land and other property.

Divorce by mutual consent of both the parties to the marriage is also permitted by custom among the *Bhot* community. A husband cannot divorce the wife without assigning any reason. Main reason for divorce is the domestic quarrels between the husband and wife. In such a situation, the village elders try to reconcile the differences between the parties, but when the parties insist on divorce, the formalities are completed and the matter ends up in divorce.

RELIGION

Lahaulas are overwhelmingly Buddhist. It is said that the Buddhism spread widely in Lahaul during the 11th century AD when the Buddhist saints established new monasteries and repaired the old dilapidated ones. The monasteries at Gumrang and Sissu were said to have been constructed during this period by a famous Buddhist and translator Rinchen Zang-po. Later in 16th century, two sub-sects in the valley came into being who have survived even today. These were Lho-Drugpa and Drugpa. Actual introduction of the Buddhism in the Lahaul and Spiti valley dates back to 8th century, believed to be by Padma

Sambhava, the famous missionary from Udyana (a place near Kashmir). According to ancient Tibetan books, Padma Sambhava visited Mandi and Lahaul during the 8th century and preached the doctrines of Buddha and it was during this time, it is said that shrines at Triloknath and Guru Ghantal were established. Previous to this, people had no fixed or proper religion and used to believe in worshipping snakes, demons and spirits etc. It is said that Triloknath temple was originally a Shiva temple and a place of pilgrimage for the Hindus. Later on, the setting up of wide marble image of *Avalokita* is attributed to Padma Sambhava of Udyana.

Though Buddhism and Hinduism are the major religions, but village deities ranging from a piece of cloth tied around a tree to totem poles with a trident on top and yaks tail hair hung aloft are also revered. Lahaul's numerous Gompas are rich store houses of Buddhist art and culture. their Lamas dominate the social fabric and no celebration, function or ritual is complete without them. Amongst the Gompas, the Kardang, Gondhla, Shashur and Guru Ghantal monasteries are the most important, while the temples of Triloknath and Mirkula Devi also attract many devotees.

LANGUAGE

People in Lahaul valley have very peculiar languages which are three in number. *Bunan* is spoken in the Bhaga valley, *Tinan* is spoken in the Chandra valley while *Manchat* is spoken in the Chandra Bhaga valley up to Thirot. All these three languages are said to have strong affinities with the languages of Munda speaking tribes of the pre-Aryan times of India. It is connected with the Tibetan only in relation to vocabulary.

FOOD AND FOOD HABITS

Lahaulas are almost non-vegetarian and their diet includes meat in one or the other way. Their staple food is barley, buckwheat, wheat, rice, potato, turnips and meat which may be taken in different combinations and as such many preparations are made out of these substances along with some other materials to change the taste and to bring variety.

Some of the common preparations are being described here:-

Ganthur

It is a kind of soup which is thick in consistency and is prepared by boiling leaves of buckwheat, cabbage, turnips and other vegetables in water and then fried in butter oil, sarson oil, fat of goat or sheep. Later it is added to butter milk and is taken with Lowads.

Lowad

Fermentation of buckwheat flour or other flour is carried out with the addition of buttermilk, sodium bicarbonate or *Phaphda* for a day or so depending upon the season (temperature). This liquid is spread over an iron pan and baked. In fact, these are baked by putting the material on the side which is towards the fire and smoke. Burning and charting of the material being baked is avoided. Both sides are baked in this way. A portion of the fermented flour can be retained for subsequent fermentation and baking since it can be used as a yeast. All the families do keep this type of yeast with them.

Tishkori

This is a coarse preparation since the husk of buckwheat and barley grains is used. This is made into a powder like flour and then kneeded and baked like a thick cake. Smoke is not used when fully baked. It is taken with vegetable, soup or curry.

Aktori

Since buckwheat is available in plenty. its leaves are boiled in water to make them soft and then these are added to buckwheat flour and kneeded like other flours. Salt to taste is also added. This material is then baked on a special iron pan. It is taken with soup or butter-milk during lunch, dinner or breakfast.

Kani

It is a preparation of rice which resembles in the method of its cooking to fried rice-*Pulao*. Rice is boiled with vegetables, mostly leafy and then fried in *ghee* or oil. Spices and condiments may be added to taste.

Phempra

It is a soup of mixed vegetables along with some rice and spices. All ingredients are boiled in water till they are soft and edible. Potato, pea, rice etc. may be mixed. This is fried when cooked.

Thungpa

Meat is chopped into small pieces so that the bones and other unwanted material is left out. It is boiled in water. When completely boiled butter milk is added. Roasted barley powder, Sattu is mixed with this soup. It is fried in oil, *ghee* or fat. Spices and condiments are added to taste and flavour. It can be taken with Lowad or Tishkori.

Trutshati

Rice is boiled in water and then pieces of potatoes and cheese are added which may be boiled with rice. Semi-solid soup or stew is fried in *ghee*, oil or fat. Spices and salt are added as per choice.

Doo-sattus

Barley broken in small pieces, equal to the size of poridge are boiled in water with some edible pieces of herbs. Salt is added to taste. It is taken with sauce or butter-oil.

Apart from these preparations, some other dishes are prepared by mixing few other things like peas, turnips, potatoes, leafy vegetables and flour of barley, buckwheat, wheat etc. There are many names for such preparations.

DRINKS

Being a snow-bound area and cut off from other portions for at least six months, different types of drinks and beverages are prepared by adding local products to suit their own needs and conditions.

Salted Tea

This is one of the most and easily available drink which is offered to all visitors, relatives, friends etc on all occasions. Butter and oil are mixed with the prepared tea in a special vessel called Doltog. Salt is added to taste. Outsiders are offered tea without salt.

Lugri, Lugdi or Chhang

It is a local brewed product which is intoxicating. It is prepared by boiling barley grains and some local herb known as

Phab in water and then fermenting the material. This is usually taken after being diluted with water according to the choice of the consumer. This is offered at almost all occasions and dances.

Arak or Sara

It is a special type of wine prepared by distilling the ingredients in the indigenous method.

There is no inhibition in taking different foods and drinks. Among the cereals, wheat, rice, barley, buckwheat and millets are used in different ways. Vegetables like potato, peas, turnip, cabbage etc are used in different ways by boiling or cooking. Pulses are used in less quantity. Butter, butter milk, butter fat, (ghee) and other oils are used for frying or mixing with other substances. Milk is also consumed in many ways like fresh milk, curd, butter milk and whey. Dried meat of sheep, goat and yak is also used. Spices, condiments and flavouring agents are also available. Sugar, gur, jaggery or other sweetening materials are also consumed by local people. Sauces of many kinds are prepared which are taken with baked cakes or *chapatis* and vegetables. Garlic, onion, cumin, coriander, ginger and asafoetida are used as per need and choice of the consumer.

FORESTRY

Nestled in the inner Himalayas and its deep valleys the Lahaul and Spiti district is dry, rugged and barren. There is not much scope for afforestation of economically useful forests. In fact, greatest problem is the conservation of soil and to prevent its erosion which is at its peak. While in parts of the Pattan Valley and lower parts of the Chandra Valley coniferous trees have been planted with some success. In the rest of the areas poplar and willow trees are the popular species for afforestation in Lahaul.

AGRICULTURE

The area for production of crops is limited due to steep valley but whatever area is available, is being used for cultivation of crops and as such agriculture is the predominant occupation in the valley. The traditional crops on the uneconomic holdings used to be barley and buckwheat and pulses, peas, oil seeds etc. These are the cash crops even today. But, however, with the opening of the vehicular roads and awareness, people have shifted from cereal crops to commercial crops like seed potatoes. Lahaul valley produces seed potato which is known for its freedom from diseases and is popular throughout the country. Before the introduction of seed potatoes *Kuth* used to be the principal commercial crop in the valley for which a research station was set up at Keylong in 1960, Vegetables have also been introduced in the valley. Hops are also grown in some parts. This is also a cash crop. The success of these crops have raised hope of economic sustainability in the families dependent upon agriculture.

INDUSTRIES

Lahaul and Spiti district never had any industry worth the name. For setting up of industry, there is no raw material available locally, further, no local expertise and no local market is available for the produce. Due to these short-comings which are natural, only household industries like carpet weaving, carding of wool and then weaving of woollen/pashmina shawls and other clothes exist. There is a carpet weaving training centre at Keylong, others are, Government Wool Spinning and Weaving Centre at Keylong with sub-centre at Janda, Government

(Pashmina) Spinning and Weaving Centre at Chhilijam in Spiti with sub-centre at Hikkam.

However, there are many Lamas who are adapt painters. Their paintings, carvings and clay models are real master pieces and the finish, indeed, immaculate.

EDUCATION

Lahaul had been quite backward in the field of education. The main reason being the lack of communications. After the independance, the Government paid attention in this direction and opened a large number of schools. According to the census of 1991, there were 124 primary, 11 middle and 14 high or higher secondary schools in Lahaul (Source, Directorate of Economics and Statistics, Himachal Pradesh, 1995). With this the situation has improved but still there is no college in Lahaul valley, thus the people have to go to Shimla, Chandigarh, Dharamsala or Delhi for the higher education.

No written literature is found in Lahaul because of the fact that for centuries the population of this area had been illiterate. Thus, most of the knowledge has been passed on from generation to generation through oral tradition which is still being preserved, though there may be some difference in language, text or other elements which is obvious due to lack of facilities for documentation.

FESTIVE SPIRIT

Festivals and fairs break the monotony of the Lahaul's hard life. Inevitably these are the occasions for community singing, dancing and feasting when the irrepressible nature of these people reveals itself. The reasons for celebrating are plenty. **Losar**, the new year festival, the birth of a son, the procession of the village deity, a marriage are to name just a few. An added attraction during festivals are the mask dances performed by the Lamas of various monasteries. Donning colourful dresses and costumes, the Lamas dance gracefully to the tunes of flutes, drums and bronze plates.

The art and craft of this land are an expression of their vibrant culture. The craftsmen create magic that transforms jade, silver and bronze into beautiful crockery and jewellery: the magic of his brush creates the *Thankas* that adore most of the Gompas: his skill creates priceless wood carvings, like the one's in the famed temples of Triloknath and Mirkula Devi.

MAJOR SOCIAL AND CULTURAL EVENTS

Traditionally in the olden days about 4-5 centuries ago, there used to be annual fairs at various places like Keylong. These fairs basically had trade significance in them and the traders from Tibet and India used to come over with the articles from their respective regions and barter used to take place. But, with the closure of border with Tibet, much of its historical significance has been lost. However, Government have been trying to encourage such fairs on Independence Day, Republic Day and other days of national importance. by introducing exhibitions and cultural events. These sponsored fairs do not seem to be ideal substitute to the traditional ones, but may be, a good substitute under the present circumstances.

Lahaul and Spiti district has good number of festivals which people celebrate with great fun, festivity and joy. In Lahaul, *Phagli, Halda* and *Gotsi* are the important festivals. Phagli is the new year festival in Pattan Valley while Halda and Gotsi or *Gochi* are the festivals of the Chandra and the Bhaga valleys celebrated in the month of February. All these festivals have religious significance as certain beliefs which the local people cherish, are fulfilled through the celebration of these festivals. Invariably, after completing the set ceremonies the festival ends with feasting with meat and *Chhang* and dancing. Since Lahaul valley had been under the invasion of one kingdom or the other, either from north or south or east or west, therefore, it had never got opportunity to develop its own culture.

CHAPTER - III
FAIRS, FESTIVALS AND CELEBRATIONS

Due to diverse cultural and social activities, Lahaul is known as *Wonderland*. Although the place remains cut off from the world for more than six months due to heavy snowfall but during some pleasant months, people spare some time to celebrate different fairs, festivals and ceremonies. They do celebrate some festivals during winter months inside their homes while others are celebrated in the open during summers.

About 90 per cent of the residents are the followers of Buddhism, as such all the festivals, celebrations, social customs and ceremonies are influenced by the Buddhist culture. These are similar to those of Laddakh and Kinnaur areas which are Lahaul's neighbouring areas.

Following festivals and fairs are observed in this district. These are bit different in their mode of celebration from the other areas due to impact of neighbouring areas particularly, the Tibet which provides a Bodh touch. Description of the most common is as follows:-

Punya

The word *Punya* a Sanskrit word means good deed done by a person or a family. In olden days, Brahmins in Lahaul used to perform this celebration. People from all the villages would come in procession to take part in the celebrations where food and other eatables were prepared ahead of the ceremony. The head priest or *Pandit* would take charge of the house of the family who would desire to celebrate. It was on the recommendation of Pandit that the celebrations were held. The main purpose was to cure somebody who is sick.

People enjoy bonfire during the day after having food etc. The celebrations are held during autumn when everybody is free after collection of harvest from the fields. Huge feast is arranged. There used to be sacrifice of goats but now it is ceremonial. People sing the songs of entertainment including the description of celebrations, right from the start of invitation to the merry making. Since it was a costly feast so probably with fall in the economic conditions and change in the attitude of people, it has almost faded away.

Runah

Like Punya, this celebration was held by people of other castes like Thakurs and scheduled castes but not by Brahmins. This was celebrated earlier in the Pattan valley where huge feasts were arranged for whole of the village and the people coming from other places. This was common with the Bodh community and the people under the influence of Buddhism. This was also performed when someone fell sick and the Lama prescribed it. During the celebrations, a Buddhist musical instrument known as *Bugjal* and a pair of drums called *Nyishan* were played by scheduled castes which was a quite unusual combination. The most conspicuous aspect was the serving of a local liquor to all the people which was given as a gift. This celebration is not held now-a-days.

Mulli

It was a symbolic worship of the Goddess Hidimba who was wife of Bhimsen, one of the Pandavas. Hidimba belonged to Kullu area and she was regarded as a demon. Her temple was built in the village of Jahlma and it is believed that the celebration was started by Raja Man Singh of Kullu who ruled this part of Lahaul from 1688 to 1719 and established the temple of Hidimba in this village. The main attraction of the celebration was the purchase of a yak by one of the worshipper family and then was let loose in the field on one Saturday and was to be caught by throwing a rope on Saturday by a scheduled caste. Then the yak was sacrificed in a peculiar way. The heart of the yak is to removed while she/he is living by tearing open the body. Later other parts of body of the yak were taken out and distributed among the fellow worshippers and others as a part of offering. People used to taste the blood of the yak. It was celebrated after every third year in the past but after the World War II, this celebration has almost abandoned.

Mani Mahesh Kailash Darshan

Mani Mahesh Kailash is a place in Bharmaur of the district Chamba. The peak of the mountain remains snow-clad almost whole of the year. In fact, the peak remains shrouded in mist and fog and no pilgrim reaches there. This is a sort of pilgrimage i.e. glimpse (*Darshan*) of Mahesh i. e. Lord Shiva. People from Lahaul go to visit this place and they usually go in groups, perhaps due to difficult path and many climatic hazards during the journey/travel. They have to cross high mountains and many passes in the midst of glaciers.

A feast is arranged for the relatives, friends and the companions participating in this *Jatra* (journey) and in the late evening *Dhoop* (incense) and cedar needles are burnt by 4 or 5 Gurus. With the smoke, it is believed that the *Gura* goes into trance and starts the *Grahni*. He may put off his clothes from the upper part of the body and then start beating himself by iron chains. He may put fire in his mouth or use a sword which is like a penance. It is further believed that God speaks through *Guru* which is regarded as a verdict or decision of God. Later the party continues where drinks and dance is a common feature.

Jagra

In the Pattan valley, there is a small Shiva temple in the village of Mayling. There is one altar in the temple but people may have many outside the main temple. These are usually covered with flowers, oil or butter as a form of worship.

For *Jagra*, the Guru, *Bhatta* or priest may fix the date for this celebration during the month of August and then huge feast is organised by the family. The reason of this celebration may be the verdict of the priest to please Lord Shiva for curing a person or some other reason. *Guras* are called upon and they go into trance one by one while the smoke is being produced as a result of the burning of *Dhoop* and cedar needles. A sheep is also sacrificed and the meat is cooked and offered as a Prasad (offerings) to the villagers.

Triloknath Fair

People of all castes and creeds would gather near this temple from far and near places. It is a combination of pilgrimage and festival. In the morning they have a *Darshan* (glimpse) of Triloknath who is the lord of three worlds. This is regarded as Avalokiteshwara by Buddhists. Hindus and Bodh both worship or pray in this temple and have *Prakarma* (round of the temple).

This may be 3 or 4 times. Wheels for prayer of Buddhists are also there. Butter oil and mustard oil is used to light the lamps in the temple. In the evening people dance in a special manner i. e. in a circle as many people can join this dance at one time. Shops and stalls are also available as they are organised for the purchase of gifts and other items of need by the villagers.

On the next morning, traditional procession is held which is headed by the Thakur of Triloknath riding a decorated horse. They go to the place where the seven angels appeared from seven springs. From here the procession returns back to the fair ground for more festivities. Generally, the fair last for 3 days, people come on the first day, worship in the procession on the second day and leave for their respective places on the third day.

Halra or Halda

Halra festival is celebrated in Gadhar valley of Lahaul. This festival is celebrated according to Buddhist rites.

This festival is celebrated every year during the end of January or the beginning of February to welcome the arrival of new year. Good wishes and prayers are offered for the happiness and prosperity of every-one. The village deity and the family deity is worshipped. The main priest or Lama of Shashur Gompa decides the day of the celebration and announces the commencement of this festival. This festival is celebrated for seven days. Alongwith the special worship of local deity many games, dances and songs are performed. The most attractive game is the playing on the snow under the torch-light which the people carry along them. People celebrate this festival in their homes since it is very cold outside and no congregation can be held. Many types of dances are performed inside the house around bonfire which makes them warm and they feel comfortable. Different types of dishes are prepared and all the family members enjoy the feast. On the seventh day, the birds are fed with the grains of cereals and millets which is the concluding ceremony of this festival.

In some areas of Lahaul it is known as *Halag* or *Khogal*. The torches are lighted by performing some rituals. It is compulsory that at least one person from each house should come out with the lighted torch to participate in the festival. Whosoever does not come out is called bad names and as such every-one takes part in the game of playing in the snow.

Kunh or Phagli

This festival is celebrated within a fortnight after Halda. On this day people offer flowers as a token of greetings for the new year. This is most common in Pattan valley. People decorate their houses at least a day prior to celebrations. They lit lights in the house as is done during the festival of lights. The head of the family and the lady prepare a dough of *Sattu* which is shaped into small balls and pyramids and taken to the roof of the house from where it is offered to deity. Another preparation, *Kawari* is thrown to crows. The offerings made for the deity are later distributed among the family members as *prasad*. And next day they pay their annual respect to cows and sheep. This is followed by paying respect to elders by bowing down before them and in return they are blessed by elders.

Gochi/Gotsi

Gochi is another important festival of the Chandra and the Bhaga valleys which is celebrated in the month of February in the houses where a son was born during the preceding year. This festival is celebrated with some variations in different villages.

The festival lasts for three days. The family which is blessed with a son, invites all relatives and friends to celebrate the happy occasion. All of them gather together in the form of a procession at a fixed place in the village. The head of the family worships the deity. All the family members and friends put on their best colourful dresses. The mother of the newly born son also performs the worship. In the lower Keylong, there is an old tree and the people of Keylong regard this tree as the local deity and worship this tree. The boys of the village bring the *"Shiva-Lingam"* made of wheat or barley flour, and is offered to the tree deity. During the three days of celebrations there are feats of bow and arrows which is a perfect form of archery. Gochi is celebrated fifteen days after the Halra festival.

At some places the replica of goat made out of ghee and flour is offered to the deity. In the past there used to be the offering or sacrifice of goat but now it is symbolic as goat prepared out of ghee is offered.

Shashur Mela

Shashur is one of the major fairs of Lahaul. Shashur is also known as *"Chheshu"*. The whole of Lahaul valley celebrates this festivals. People from other adjoining districts also come here to participate in this fair. It is celebrated during the end of June or beginning of July. During the festival, the famous dance-drama is enacted by the monks dressed in colourful costumes and masks. On the first day of the fair Devil Dance is organised. It is a famous dance of Lahaul. In this dance, the Lamas perform the dance by putting on various masks. It is a mask dance and the main mask is of the Devil. That is why it is known as Devil Dance. On the second day, the dance is performed around *"Chhortan"* which is the typicality of this fair. It is a traditional dance. With the performance of this dance the fair comes to an end. In some places they also recite the hymns from the holy book written in Bhoti language.

Dongza

Dongza festival is celebrated to pay homage to a chief Lama who attained salvation on this day. All the people of the village get together and celebrate the death anniversary of the very honourable Lama. It is believed that this Lama used to perform many miracles. It is also customary to celebrate many types of festivities and ceremonies during winter months, since, it becomes quite difficult to go outside due to heavy snowfall. Moreover the agricultural activities are also at stand still during these months. In order to pass the time and break the monotony of daily routine, people of Lahaul always find one or the other pretext to get together and enjoy through dance, music and festivities. Dongza is also a such type of festival. No songs are sung in this festival.

Tambariya

Tambariya is a religious festival. People perform worship and sit together at a place fixed by the head priest. The process of worship continues for seven or eight days. The typical Lahauli "*Ghure*" are sung. These songs are of historical and mythological themes. The recitation of Ghure are a must during these days of Tambariya. Young boys and girls perform many types of dances and enjoy singing. Usually the songs are of religious theme. Due to winters this festival is celebrated inside the house. Thus the dances are of slow movements.

Utana or Lohri

On the 13th January every year Utana festival is celebrated. On this day the Lahauli New Year starts. It is just like the Lohri festival in the other parts of the state and in most parts of Lahaul it is known as *Lohri*. Due to severe winters during January, a big bonfire is arranged. People sing and dance around bonfire. Many eatables are prepared and exchanged. A special function is held at Triloknath Temple, the deity is given the holy bath on this day.

Losar or Kunh

This is one of the major festivals of Lahaul which is held sometimes in November or December and lasts for 3 days. Many days before the actual festival, the preparations are started. During the festival people visit each other's house. They are welcomed with great joy and happiness. They adore their caps with special flowers. The abundant use of local drink is the marked activity of this festival.

Yore

Fifteen days after Kunh another festival, Yore is celebrated. Those who could not visit each other during Kunh, do it during "Yore" festival. This festival is celebrated in Triloknath village. People from every part of Lahaul come here and meet each other. They enjoy a lot of local drink. This festival is a welcome to the spring season which is expected after this festival.

Chaitrori

Chaitrori is a festival which is connected with the agricultural activities. It is celebrated on the first day of the month of *Chaitra* corresponding to 15th Marth. During winter, a heavy layer of snow accumulates in the fields. On the first day of Chaitra, people prepare their fields for sowing of crops. They put soil on top of the snow so that it may melt soon and they may sow the seeds for the new harvest. Chaitrori is a ritual connected with such of type of agricultural activities.

Baisakhi

Baisakhi is also a seasonal festival. The change of season is welcomed. Many types of eatables are prepared. Songs and dances performed by young boys and girls add to the gaiety of this festival.

Diwali or Khogal

Diwali, the festival of light is celebrated on the full moon day of the month of *Magh*, corresponding to January. It is also known as Khogal in some parts. People play on the snow with lighted torches. The play goes on till late night. The local drink or wine is also consumed on large scale.

Chapter IV
FOLK LORES

The term folk lore refers to the mythology and legend which were handed over from generation to be reproduced to writing and constituted the cultural background of the country and its people. The term Lore refers to the materials of folklore rather than the people who use the materials. It has been described in terms of origin, form, transmission and function. And the means for transmission of folklore is said to be in "Oral tradition". It appears that folk-lore is transmitted from individual to individual, often directly by word or act, at times being copied from another artist even without personal contact.

According to Richard M Dorson, "the traditional concept from its initial conceptualization, folklore outlines the hidden, forgotten and ancient culture. This culture of the folk was hidden in two ways, (i) deep in remote time in a prehistoric past when early man perceived the world animalistically, or at least in the pre-Christian era when pagan man indulged in barbarous rites, and (ii) in far off places away from the busy centres of civilization in the peasant villages of the country side and mountain ridges." It is now well established that the most civilized races have all fought their way slowly upwards from a condition of savagery. Now, savages can neither read nor write yet they manage to collect and store up a considerable amount of knowledge of a certain kind. The knowledge, organisation and the rules thus gathered and formulated are preserved in the memory and communicated by word of mouth and by actions of various kinds. To this mode of preservation and communication as well as to the things thus preserved and communicated, the name of tradition is given to folklore as the Science of Tradition.

The forms of folklore are the myths, legends, folk-arts and crafts, ballads, beliefs, charms, customs, dance and drama, folk tales, folk songs and fables etc. Folklore is a study of culture and as a form of expression through the music, the dance or the drama. It is a part of man's learned traditions and customs, a part of his social heritage. It can be analyzed in the same way as other customs and traditions in terms of form and function or of inter-relations with other aspects of culture. Lahauli folklore is also the index of its culture. Who were the original inhabitants of this region and what was the form of their culture? These questions are very difficult to answer. Yet it is sure that the age-old traditions and customs are still practised by the people of this region.

The study of history of Lahaul is the proof that the culture of this region has been influenced by the Bhot from the east and by the Aryan culture from the south. All these civilizations have been intermixing thus, resulting in the mixed tradition of celebrating the religious and social customs, rituals, beliefs and fairs and festivals. The style of celebrating cannot be connected with any particular sect, religion or caste. The folklores confirm these facts.

The folklores are mostly sung or narrated. They reflect the age-old culture and traditions. Mythological beliefs and customs are also evident from these tales. A peculiar aspect of the preservation of these tales are the rituals which are performed before a folklore is narrated or sung. A folklorist has to observe many formalities. First of all before starting the actual narration he must worship the village deity and chant the mantras. He must worship with the offering of the leaves of Cidar (Devdar), flowers, ghee and barley and perform "Havan Yajna". He must chant the Mantra "*Oma huyulla tete khen*". or "*Chho chhod leyi gayanpon tanjar tete khjen*" etc. and afterwards he must finish the ritual traditionally, only then he can start the narrations of the folklore. The traditional lores are known as Ghure. A few popular tales are being documented here.

STORIES ABOUT THE PANDAVAS

Looking at the mythological and historical stories, there are several stories about Lord Shiva and the Pandavas in Lahaul. Studies reveal that the local myths and stories are neither totally baseless nor blindly fabricated by the local people, instead there are specific scriptural backgrounds to most of the stories. For example, the Shiva Purana is full of stories of Shiva's being in that area. Similarly, in the Mahabharata it is stated that the Pandavas went to the Himalaya on their last journey.

In the epic Mahabharata, it is mentioned that after their victory over the Kauravas and regaining their throne, the Pandavas did not find solace or happiness and peace of mind. They blamed themselves for the destruction of the country, and the death of many people, including many of their own kins. So they handed over the throne to their grandson Prikshit and left on a pilgrimage to the Himalayas. This was their last journey, they died one by one on their way to Himalayas, until only Yudhistra, the eldest brother, was left alive. Then of Indra appeared on his chariot, which took him straight to Heaven. It is also believed that Draupadi, the wife of the Pandavas, died in Lahaul at Tandi.

The myth about the formation of Rohtang Pass by a kick from Bhimsen, the second of the Pandava brothers, is also narrated in Lahaul valley.

Many strange objects, incidents and occurrences are attributed to the Pandavas. There is a song also, which describes the strange characteristics during the time of the Pandavas, the first few lines of this song are as follows:-

Jab thiye Panduru re raj
Tab thiye nou gaja mahnu
Jab thiye Panduru re raj
Tab thiye hathi re ghora
Jab thiye Panduru re raj
Tab thiye ghora re seenga
Jab thiye Panduru re raj
Tab thiye sat gaja janana

According to the song during the reign of the Pandavas, the men stood nine yards tall and the women seven yards tall. Also, the horse were as large as elephants and they had horns. The lice were as big as lizards and single grain of wheat weighed one seer (over two pounds). In whole of the song there is the description of such strange objects. It seems that the songs is just a symbolic representation of the Pandavas greatness.

MYTHS ABOUT THE RIVER CHANDRA-BHAGA

According to a common story, Chandra was the daughter of the Moon and Bhaga was the son of Sun God. They were in love and wanted to get married. With this intention they went to the top of Bara Lacha pass. They decided to run from this pass in opposite directions, encircling the vast tract of the Himalaya to meet again in Tandi for their eternal union. With this promise and hope they set off running, Chandra heading south and Bhaga north. Chandra was smart and swift, even though she had a greater distance to cover, she reached Tandi before Bhaga. Not finding her lover there, she became anxious and worried and headed towards Bhaga valley in search of her lover. From a distance she saw Bhaga coming slowly and struggling through the rocks. When Bhaga reached the fixed place both performed their celestial marriage and this place is called Sangam which means union. It is the same point where the Chandra and the Bhaga rivers unite. As a matter of fact at the junction of two rivers, one can actually see that the Chandra river, the right bank curls up towards the left, that is the Bhaga river, before they join. According to another legend it is said that long ago, Lahaul used to be the abode of the Rishis (saints). They came in large numbers to this holy spot for meditation and had hermitages built along the rivers Chandra and the Bhaga, in which flowed milk instead of water. During those days, the rivers did not tumble through narrow gorges but ran smoothly through grassy green plateaus. Sitting in meditation every morning, the sages would drink a cup of milk from the river even before opening their eyes.

Demons came to know about this wonderful land and the sages living there. They became jealous. To create hindrance in the *Samadhi* of the sages, the demons killed a number of animals and threw them in at the source of the rivers. As usual, the sages ended their meditation with a drink of milk from the river without looking at it. That day it tasted different. They found the rivers running with blood instead of milk. The Rishis were upset by having their life-long efforts of meditation being waisted by the sin of drinking blood and then left the valley forever. Out of anger, they also left a curse that the rivers from then on, would run in deep gorges and that no one would drink their water or use it for any other purpose. So the water of these rivers became unusable.

Actually the rivers are running in deep gorges, making it impossible to use their water for irrigation or any other purpose without considerable effort, and also the water remains muddy most of the time and is not suitable for drinking.

LORE ABOUT THE ESTABLISHMENT OF TRILOKNATH TEMPLE

Triloknath is an important place of pilgrimage in Pattan valley. This temple is built on the pattern designed by Lalitaditya of Kashmir during 725-726 A.D. Most of the portion of the present temple is of much later period.

There are so many presumptions that this Shiva temple was transformed into Buddhist shrine but according to its present image of Avalokiteshwara Triloknath, it is a fact that this temple is sacred to both Buddhists and Hindus alike. There is a legend about the establishment of Triloknath temple. It is believed that no-body has installed the idol of Triloknath but it has itself emerged. Once a shepherd named Tindanu was passing through the village Hindsa. He listened a voice calling him and asking to take him to Triloknath. Tindanu stopped and to his great surprise he found that the stone idol of Shiva, the Triloknath was lying near the rock. On the instruction of the idol, the shepherd carried it on his back and brought it in Triloknath village and installed it there. Later, a splendid temple was erected at the place where the idol was installed. The people sing the Ghure song in connection with this story and is also sung on the auspicious occasions and during the Pauri festival at Triloknath. The beginning lines of this Ghure are as follows.

Tindanu puhala he hinseri grave ji ho
Tindanu puhala he bheda bakari chari ji ho
Bheda bakari vo niji murti re dhara ji ho
Niji murti vo dungeri gothe ji ho
Tindanu puhala he sukheya sutora ji ho
Sata murti he khel khilade ji ho

It is a long song describing the discovery of idol and then its establishment at Triloknath. People also believe that during those days the idol used to speak. At a place called Maing Dhar, there used to be seven idols playing on the river side. These idols were made of marble. Tindanu Puhal, the shepherd happened to pass through that Dhar. He was surprised to see the idols playing and speaking. He hid himself and began to watch the play. He also gave them milk and curd. He caught one of the idols and served him nicely. The idol became happy with the service of the shepherd, so asked the shepherd to request for a boon and told him that he is Triloknath and asked him to take it to the village and install it in the temple. So Tindanu Puhal carried the idol on his back and brought it to its present place. Whatever, may be the legend, it is a fact that there is a temple which is the last wooden temple built in the tradition of the early 8th century. The present image of Avalokitshwara cannot be earlier than that of 12th century. During 1569-70 the silver idol of goddess Kali in her form as Mahishasurmardini was installed.

STORY ABOUT THE DEVIL LHEBE

Lhebe was a devil who lived on a hill across the river Chandra in the Gondhla valley. He created havoc for the people living nearby. They were afraid of Lhebe even during the day while walking alone in that area. One day a powerful Buddhist Lama was passing through, riding a horse. Lhebe came, climbed up on the back of his horse behind the Lama. The Lama removed his Zangoi-a cloth used by the Lamas to wrap around like shawl and tied the devil with it, along with himself and drove the horse as fast as he could. With his spiritual powers, the Lama made Lhebe totally helpless before him. He then took the devil to his house. There he removed Lhebe's Godiri, his outer jacket, buried it under the fire place, reciting some Mantras which prevented Lhebe from removing it. The Godiri bound Lhebe to the Lama's house. He could neither leave it behind, nor could be remove it from beneath the fire place, because of the powerful Mantras protecting it. The Lama then used Lhebe as a slave, to do all types of hard labour. When sent to the forest to collect firewood, Lhebe returned with whole trees, piling them up in front of the house.

One day, the Lama went to a fair in a nearby village. Lhebe found a chance to run away, but not without his Godiri. He enticed the Lama's old mother to place her hand on the fire place as the Mantra would not affect Lhebe while her hand touched the fire place, and so he was able to lift the stones and remove his Godiri beneath the fire-place. Next he removed the old woman's heart and set off for the fair. When the Lama saw the heart in Lhebe's hand who also had his Godiri on, he immediately came to knew what must have happened. He quickly ran home and found his mother dead and chased Lbehe, but could not catch him again. From that day on, Lhebe never dared to come around and bother people. He left for good and everyone breathed a sigh of relief. The people of Lahaul valley sing this story and narrate them to their children.

SONG OF OLIYAS RANA

O Liya Seri Rana, bara mangune aye
Handi na pheri ye, ma dangeri sare
Thari na veni ye, chadi re ghare
jara bhimi Rama, poochhane lagi
O Liya seri Rana, kiji kame aye
Tendune dive, bara mangune aye
Jada bhimi Rama, appu raji bhuye
Triji barsushe O, byah oto kiti
O Liya seri Rana, pagudi dere
Ladi na dhuni ye, rolune lagi
Chhuti O mendurne, mayi na babu
Chhuti O mendurne, bhaya na bahini
Chhuti O mendurne, sanga na sugi
Chhuti O mendurne, mandugeri house
Bhai na babu, shikha vo ditti
Roye matu divaye, bhale jogu biyahe
Bhaleri dive, bhale jogu biyahe

This song is sung during the wedding ceremony and is popular in Lahaul in connection with the marriage of the daughter. The description of the folklore is as follows. Oliyas Rana roamed about in the villages in search of a bride for himself. At last he reached Modunga village. He went from door to door in order to find a beautiful bride. He reached to a house and straight away went up the stairs of the house. An old man was sitting there and he asked the Rana who he was. He said that he is Oilyas Rana. The old man asked him the purpose of his visit to his house.

Oliyas Rana told that he has come to this place to marry the daughter of the old man. The old man whose name was Bhimi Ram happily agreed to get his daughter married to Oliyas Rana.

Oliyas Rana was also very pleased to have a beautiful lovely bride. He got married and started back to his place along with his bride. He was feeling very proud.

The bride whose name was Dhooni sat in the palanquin to go to her husband's place and was feeling very sad to leave her parent's house. She started crying on knowing that her parents were being left there. They have brought me up and loved me dearly. My brothers and sisters have also been left here. All my friends are no longer my companions. I am feeling very sad and she started crying bitterly.

Her parents advised her that eventually every daughter has to go to her husband's place. O my dear daughter, you are very lucky because you have got a gentle, handsome and rich husband. You yourself are very nice, honest and beautiful, and have got a good husband. Do not cry and go to your husband's house. He is a good person and will keep you with care and love. It is the destiny of every girl to go to her husband's house sooner or later.

WAZIR RAM SNEHI/RAMU SAI

Wazir Ram Snehi was the resident of the Chembak village. He used to live in the royal style due to his position as a tax collector. These tax collectors were known as Wazir. They enjoyed very prestigious position in the court of the king. During those days, Lahaul was under the regime of king of Kullu valley.

The people of Lahaul still sing the life-style of Wazir Ram Snehi. This song has attained the status of Ghure.

The text of this folk lore is as follows:-

Part I

Bari e wazira e bari teri naven

Bari e wazira a bari teri mesari

Bari e wazira e bari teri mesari

Bari e wazira e bari teri prauri

E Prauri upuru e siya mukha likhi

E Prauri upuru e rishi muni likhi

E Prauri upuru e panja pandya likhi

E Prauri upuru e surja chanduri likhi

Tate e upuri e appu narena likhi

Bari e zazira e bari teri prauri

E Sabe Ramu sai chaura putura jami

E Chaura putura e eke ranga roope

E Chaura putura e baturi re veera

E Chaura putura e vara lori manguna

Part II

E Thahri na beeni e jhunderi graven

A Andi na pheri e bamuneri dhare

E Sehna bamuna e edure rakhi

E Sehna bamuna e punchhuni lagi

E Sabe Ramu sai kiji kame aye

E Sabe Ramu sai kiji kame aye

E Jiya mere sahibaye nusha manguna aye

E Tenduna dheeva a nusha manguna aye

E Bamuna bamuni e samyuna kiti

E Bamuna bamuni e mane raji bhuye

E Bamuna bamuni e shaguna kiti

E Bamuna bamuni e shaguna kiti

E Tiji barushe e byah-oto kiti

E dheeva sulaki e byah-oto kiti

E Deeva sulaki e roluni lagi

E Mai na babu e shikha budhi diti
Roye matu dheeva e suthahri byahiye
Roye matu otheeva e bhale jogu byahiye
Baso dheeva sulaki e chemba keri thahriye
Chemba keri thahri e suthah ri bol iye

Wazir Ramusai was a prosperous man who lived with great pomp and show. O Wazir! your house is as big as is your name. It is said that the great personalities have good things also. You have a very large mansion. The hall of your mansion is also as big as is your house. The pillars of the hall are decorated with the carvings of lions and the images of gods and deities. On the ceiling of the hall, the images of saints and seers have been carved and on one side there is the painting of five Pandavas. The upper portion of the hall is decorated with the images of Lord Vishnu and Lakshmi along with seven snake gods. In the same manner on the top of the hall, sun and moon have been carved with thousand rays. On top of the mansion, the image of lord Vishnu is carved.

O Wazir Ramu Sai, in fact the hall of your house is really very glorious. In due course of time Ramu Sai Wazir was blessed with four sons. All the four sons were very handsome and were very well-behaved. Ramu Sai Wazir wanted to get his four sons married to beautiful girls. All the four sons of Wazir Ramu Sai turned out to be very brave men and warriors. So Wazir Ramu Sai wanted the brides according to the status of his sons. Moreover, he wanted to perform the wedding during his life-time since he had become quite old. He discussed the matter with his relatives and expressed his desire. Eventually he set out in search of the brides who could become his daughters-in law.

Everybody wished that the girls should be beautiful, obedient and cultured. Ramu Sai thought that he should be very careful in selecting the brides, otherwise all his respect will dash to the grounds. He was worried about this but he went on from one village to another. He found that the climate and season of each place effects the personality. So he also thought over this aspect and continued his journey. At last he reached a village called Jhunda. This village was situated away from the main road. He was much pleased to see the natural scenic beauty of the village. He thought that he could get the desired brides in this village because the village was so beautiful and as such the inhabitants must also be beautiful. Although Wazir Ramu Sai had reached the Jhunda village but he was quite ignorant about the villagers. He reached in the middle of the village and saw a few elderly persons sitting on the platform and discussing their domestic problems. The wazir enquired about the village and accordingly went inside the palatial house of a Brahmin family.

All the members of the family were surprised to see the richest and most respected person as a guest in their house. They heartily welcomed the Wazir and offered dainty dishes. Then the old Brahmin asked the Wazir the purpose of his visit to his house so that he may do accordingly.

The Wazir politely replied that he wanted his daughter to be as his daughter-in-law. He was little bit hesitant but again requested the old Brahmin to accept his offer and get his daughter married to his son. The Brahmin and his wife discussed the matter. They were highly elated to get the offer for their daughter from such a respectable family, but due to the fear and formality they were unable to accept the offer, though within heart of their hearts they were happy to accept the offer.

They finished the formalities and asked the permission of their family deity. Finding some good omen they announced that they had happily accepted the offer but the marriage will be solemnised after three years. The Wazir also kept the word and after three years the marriage was solemnised in the proper Rajput style. At the time of the departure, the girl Sullakhi started crying and said that she is leaving behind her dear parents, her village and her friends and is going to unknown place among the unknown people.

The parents of Sullakhi advised her dear daughter to not to cry since she was going to a very respectable and noble family. She had been married to a gentle, brave and handsome person Everybody praised the beauty of Chembak village which is now your in-laws place. It is a matter of great pride for us that you got good parents-in-laws. So do not cry and happily go to your house, which is your real place. Your in-laws are now your parents. You serve them with great care and abide by their advises. This is the law of the nature and every girl has to go to her in-laws house after marriage.

The village Chembak was illuminated profusely on this occasion. Wazir Ramu Sai was also very happy in getting a lovely, beautiful and obedient daughter-in-law. He spent rest of his life peacefully.

But as the fate would have it, the Chembak village lost all his glory after the death of Wazir Ramu Sai. This splendid house also turned into ruins. These days not even a single memoirs is found in Chembak village. But the tradition of adding the surname of Wazir is still prevalent among the generation of Wazir Ramu Sai's family and they are still preserving the tradition of their family.

CHAPTER - V
MUSICAL INSTRUMENTS

Musical instruments possess an important place in the folk music of Lahaul. Especially all types of songs are accompanied by the instruments, except "*Ghure*", the traditional historical and mythological songs. Ghure are sung without the accompaniment of instruments.

Out of the four categories of instruments, only three types of instruments are in vogue for the accompaniment of songs and dances. At times, solo playing of these instruments is also in practice but mostly they are played to the accompaniment of songs and dances. The string instruments are not found in Lahaul.

Following are the popular instruments.

(i) Membranophonic or Percussion instruments - *Dholak, Nagara* and *Paun.*

(ii) Ideophonic or Struck instruments - The metal disc or *Thali.*

(iii) Aerophonic or Wind instruments - Flute, *Shank, Kahal, Ransingha.*

These days the drums have also become popular. Previously only the community of blacksmiths and *Hessis* used to play these instruments but now everyone whosoever is capable of playing can play it. A very traditional and ancient instrument known as "*Rigole*" is just like but Nagara it has become extinct these days.

Membranophonic or Percussion Instruments

Dholak

This is the most common instrument used to keep the rhythm and time. Dholak is popular throughout India and it is the favourite instrument of the folk people. The Dholak which is used in Lahaul's folk music is 3 ft long and about of 6 inches in diameter. Its body is made of wood. Both the sides are covered with animal hide and to stretch the hide there are strings in which rings are threaded. By pulling the ring, the hide is stretched and it produces the sound in high pitch. It adds to the melody of the music. It is played with both the hands.

Nagara

Nagara is also an important and popular instrument which is used for many purposes like for sending some message and, for the worship of local deity or for the accompaniment of music to keep rhythm and time.

Nagara consists of two parts. Both the parts are covered with hide of the animals. They appear like big bowls, Both the parts are played either with hand or with a stick. Sometimes one part is played with hands and the other by the sticks. These two parts are known as "*Chhaj* and *Ghuma*".

Paun

Paun is a typical instrument of Lahaul. Though it looks like a *Dholak* but is quite different from it. It is broader on both the sides but the middle part is narrower than the sides. Both the sides of Paun are covered with hide. On one side of the Paun, there are little strings which serve as the tuning fork. The other part is used far playing. It is played by rubbing the fingers on the hide and this produces a very melodious sound. This instrument is not used for keeping the time but is used to add melody to the atmosphere. Usually it is played during the fairs, festivals or other happy occasions.

Ideophonic or Struck Instruments

Thali

Only one such instrument is found in Lahaul and that is the domestic utensil, a bronze plate known as *Thali*. It is not used to keep the time or to provide rhythm but it is played in a typical style while doing witch-craft such as taking out the poison of snake bite etc. The priest and other people sing songs while the witch-craft is going on. At that occasion the *Thali* is struck in a particular style and it looks like as if the rhythm is being provided for the accompaniment to the song or dance.

Aerophonic or Wind Instruments

Flute (Bansuri)

The most popular and liked by all is the flute which every Lahaula can very well play. The whole of Lahaul valley resounds with the sweet and melodious tunes of flute. The flute which is popular in Lahaul is just like the normal flute that is used to accompany the folk music in any other part of India.

Shank or Conch

This is used on special occasions. Usually, it is blown at the time of worship in the temples and on some other auspicious occasions.

The Conch is also played on the death of an elderly person and while the funeral procession is going and is blown till the procession reaches the cremation ground. The style of blowing the conch at both the occasions is quite different and people come to know the sad or happy occasion on the basis of the blowing technique of the conch.

Kaha

Kaha is another wind instrument which is quite similar to normal Karnal but is different in size and shape.

This instrument is 1 m long with a straight hollow pipe. One end is quite broad and similar to *Dhatura* flower while the other end is quite narrow. Only two notes can be got through this instrument. Kaha is made of metal usually brass. This instrument is used during the fairs, festivals and the procession.

Ransingha

Ransingha is made of sliver or bronze. The instrument consists of two parts which are joined together. Both the parts are of the shape of English alphabet C. One part is thicker and broader than the other part. While joining the parts, each part is joined at the back thus, its shape comes out to be like the letter S. The wind is blown with great force which enables it to bring out a sound through the narrower and thinner end. Only one or two notes can be obtained through this instrument.

CHAPTER - VI
FOLK DANCES

Lahaul region remains snow covered for six to eight months. Mostly people remain in their homes for most of the time. In order to pass their time they celebrate a number of ceremonies during these months. Fairs and festivals are held during the summer months which are celebrated outside in the spacious places. In all these ceremonies, fairs and festivals, there is a great feast of songs and dances. Even agricultural operations are depicted and acted through the performance of dances and singing songs. There is a marked difference in the movements which are restricted to small and little stretched positions in the dances which are performed inside the houses but the dances performed outside are vigorous with wider movements and fast footwork. The main characteristics of these dances are that they are performed by forming a circle.

In Lahaul, mostly the dances are performed by men and women separately. Traditionally, dancing by women, particularly with men or in their presence, is considered to be below the dignity of respectable women. However, lately it has been noticed that women are also taking part quite frequently. It is being taken as a mark and part of modernization. Whenever, people find time, they gather for a dance which is usually separate for men and women.

There are some professional musicians and dancers called "Hessies". They are also called *Betas* They are a kind of nomad tribe whose livelihood is entirely dependent on singing, dancing or playing the instruments at special occasions such as weddings and worshipping etc. They generally use the same steps and dancing procedures. However, sometimes they try to copy popular music, songs and dances from the movies.

Musical instruments are played during dances. The traditional music of Lahaul which usually has four to six instruments is mostly heard at religious and community festivals. It is a weird combination of trumpets, some almost two and a half metre in length, conch shells, horns, cymbals, gongs, flutes and the beating of drums.

Common folk dances are:-

CHHAM OR DEVIL DANCE

This is a religious dance normally performed in Gompas. The dancers are dressed in bright and gaily coloured special costumes and gorgeous masks of different animals, birds and demons. The dancers follow repetitive patterns with rhythmical stamping of feet and show movement laterly in a circle. The embroidered banners and the picturesque movements of the dancers mingled with the humour of baffons create a fantastic, unforgettable and most unusual experience for the visitors. Colours that predominate in this dance are turquoise, blue, scarlet, green, yellow and pink. Normally Lamas take part in it and chant *Mantras* as the dance proceeds.

Usually this dance is performed during the celebrations of Shashur fair in the Lahaul valley. This festival is celebrated by the whole community. People from all over the valley collect at a place near the Gompa and perform the dance. The Lamas perform the Devil dance all around the Gompa near Chhatrari. It is a very traditional dance and every ritual is observed while performing it.

GRIPHI

It is a group dance performed jointly by men and women. The dancers move in a circle with the beating of the drums and the playing of flutes. The dance is accompanied by collective singing by the dancers themselves. Musicians stand apart and play on their respective instruments. The costumes are largely woollen, comprising of a pyjama and a skirt like garment for men. Women drape a shawl over their upper garments. Scarves and caps complete the ensemble. All dancers wear shoes either of grass or highly embroidered or knitted wool.

TAMBARIYA

Tambariya festival is celebrated in Lahaul for seven or eight days. The people gather together at one place and perform puja and recite religious scriptures. The young boys and girls perform this dance accompanied by religious, mythological or historical songs. These songs are known as "*Dhareksa*" but popularly known as "Ghure". The traditional instrument, *Nagara* is played for keeping the rhythm. Flute is also played for accompaniment to the songs.

SHON DANCE

This dance is without music but with stamping of feet and slow movement and with linking arms in a circle. It is an important dance which is performed during Losar festival, which is observed on the New Year. It is celebrated during *Chaitra-Vaishakh* corresponding to March and April.

CHHODPA DANCE

It is a pantomine performance with masks and is performed with the beating of drums. The dance is a functional dance with passages of mime and other sequences which are purely abstract. Slow movements with soft knee dips, with accentuation of torso is the key motif of this dance.

DANCES RELATED TO AGRICULTURAL OPERATIONS

The Lahaulas observe certain ceremonies mostly of religious nature in connection with the preparation of their fields for sowing of crops and related operations. A Lama names the auspicious day on which ploughing should be commenced (this day falls always between 8th and 22nd May). After the fields have been ploughed and the seeds sown, a procession goes round all the fields, preceeded by one or two Lamas and two drummers. At the same time some of them carry several large religious books on their backs. The whole group sits down in the field near the villages, and feasts on cakes and Chhang, supplied jointly by all the landholders. The people also join the community dances. Thus the ceremony is observed while singing and dancing. The dancers recreate through movements depicting all the agricultural operations of sowing and reaping the harvest.

SHAINI DANCE

Shaini is a slow dance, with prescribed steps and rhythm, which everybody must follow. In this ancient and traditional dance, performed to the accompaniment of "*Ghure*", people from an open circle holding hands with the alternate person, linked in a kind of circular chain. It looks like a square dance, but the steps are very peculiar which sometimes look like the fox-trot. The dancers sway back and forth and side to side. Sometimes, the hands are left free to clap with the rhythm. This was the only traditional dance in which women also took part along with men. Often only the older women would participate, the younger ones not daring to mix with men and dance.

This dance has become almost extinct today. The present generation has perhaps never tried it or even seen it being performed.

Popular Dance

A free style dance is very popular. There are no rules, regulations or set steps to be followed during the dance. Unlike western dances there are no pairs in this dance. Each dancer is by himself in the crowd. All dancers try to dance to the rhythm of the music using his own steps and movements. In earlier times this dance was generally performed to the song called Pangwal Geet. The music was provided by a *Dholaki*, a two sided drum, accompanied by a flute. Sometimes, the music alone was used without any singing, In that case the instruments would include a few flutes, Dholakis, a pair of bronze plates like cymbals, or sometimes a pair of Nissan or Nagara (a pair of drums beaten with sticks). There are several different Ragas for various occasions. They are known as *Biyahon Raga*, especially for weddings, *Dari Raga*, specifically for a celebration called "*Darri jatra*" which are performed to please Lord Shiva, and "*Gujung Raga*" specifically for processions.

This dance is usually performed by men only. Recently a band similar to the school marching band, consisting of a set of drums, a few flutes etc. has become quite common. These days women are also participating in this dance quite frequently.

GARPHI

Traditionally Garphi is a dance performed by men only. It is performed both outside as well as inside the house. When the dance is performed outside the house, it is almost like the 'Nati' dance where the dancers form the circle and dance by holding the hands of each other. Sometimes the hands are let loose and then again the circle is formed by holding the hands and a set sequence is followed including the leaning backword, forward and from left to right. It is a community dance. When the Garphi which is performed inside the house, only two male dancers perform it with unrestricted movements of hands and feet. Sometimes girls also join them. These days it is performed jointly by men and women. The composition of Lahauli dance songs are set to four, three or seven beat *Talas*. The tempo is medium. When the four beat *Tala* is played in medium tempo, the *Bols* played can be notated as follows:-

1	2	3	4		5	6	7	8
dha	gin	dha	dhin		ta	gin	ta	tin
x					0			

OR

1	2	3	4		5	6	7	8
dha	gi	ta	tin		dha	nak	dhin	na
x					0			

DASHANVI

This dance is performed by men and women jointly during the months of December-January. The dancers form the circle by holding the hands of the third person from right. In the same manner every dancer is locked like the beads in a thread. In a set sequence of footwork the dancers dance on the beat of the drum. The drummer sits inside the circle and keeps the time.

A special folk tune is played on the instruments. The instrumentalists called *Bajantris* also sit inside the circle to play the tune befitting the dance. Sometimes *Thali* is also used as a musical instrument. A special Lahauli instrument *Paun* is used to set a special sound effect which fills the atmosphere with the sense of joy and happiness. It creates the required environment for the festive dance. *Shehnai* which is known as *Surnai* in Lahaul is also a part of the instruments played.

Men and women put on costumes especially made for this dance. The costume of women consists of the following items:-

1. Katar- Long cloak till knee length usually of brown colour. It has flairs in the lower part.

2. Jacket - A special type of jacket is worn over the Katar

3. Chhir - A sash is tied around the waist, and is made of woollen cloth, usually of brown colour. It is a 20 to 30 cm broad and three metres long piece. It is also called *Gachi*.

4. Sunthana - It is a *churidar payajama*. It is usually made of gray woollen cloth.

5. Jarawahre - Woollen socks with floral knitted designs.

6. Pullan - Shoes made of special grass. These are embroidered with multi-coloured threads.

7. Round Cap - It is of red colour with black border. Flowers are also tucked in it.

8. White scarf - Used to cover the head and hangs on the shoulders.

The ladies also adore themselves with jewellery which consists of the following items:-

1. Badi - A special ornament which is worn on the head and hangs down till the cheeks.

2. Necklace - Har, worn around the neck.

3. Sahri - Long hanging ear-rings made of silver.

4. Khundu - Small ear-rings which are worn on the outer sides of the ear. These are also made of silver.

5. Bumani - A special ornament made of silver used to cover the breast.

6. Gou - A special ornament made either of gold or silver is worn over the braid and hangs down till the waist.

7. Guhithab - Golden ring studded with precious stone.

8. Nang - Thick bracelets made of silver.

The costume of men dancers consists of the following items:-

1. Pohadu/Tobudu - It is a cap similar to the Kinnauri woollen cap. The woollen cloth for this cap is imported from Tibet and is stitched like the Kullu cap. But it is slightly thinner in the middle. Usually the priests put it.

2. Chodu - A long white woollen coat. These days only a short coat is worn.

3. Churidar Pyjama - A woollen tight *Pyajama* which is bit loose than the one worn by women.

4. Gachi/Chhir - Used to tie at the waist.

5. Jarawahre - Woollen socks.

6. Pullan - Woollen shoes made of a special grass.

The men also put on Khundu, Birdali and Murki as ear-rings.

CHAPTER- VII
FOLK MELODIES

Lahauli folk songs are of different types. They are in different dialects. The people of Lahaul migrated from several different places at different times, all bringing different dialects of their own, thus, the use of such dialects is quite apparent in Lahauli folk songs.

A few songs are composed in pure Lahauli dialect but others are mixture. Some are in Kullavi, Chambyali and even broken or spoken Hindustani. Though these songs are of different themes but *Ghure*, *Pangwal Geet* and *Sugili* are quite common.

Ghure

Ghure is essentially a folk song of the ballad type depicting either a historical or a mythological story. As a matter of fact Ghure have been very helpful in tracing and researching the history of Lahaul. Very rarely is a written document of the past maintained. If any account of the valley's history was kept, it was in the form of Ghures. Among them are the accounts of the temple of Triloknath, the monastery of Guru Ghantal, the Ranas of Ghushal, the sacrifice of Rupi Rani, and the Wazir of Chambak. On the mythological aspect there are Ghure about Lord Shiva and Goddess Parvati, the sun, the moon and the Rahu (the lunar node). There are also the stories from the Ramayana and the Mahabharata which are narrated in the form of Ghure.

It is noteworthy that all the Ghure are in dialect of Kullu, Also most of them have a similar tune. Generally one group sings a line and the other group repeats the same line. Ordinarily they are sung while sitting, except for those used in the marriage procession when these are sung while walking. They are not used for ordinary dance music, but there are special dances which accompany the Ghure. Shini dance (which is almost extinct) is an example.

Ghures are composed in Kulluvi dialect but it is a very strange fact, that Ghures are not sung in Kullu. It indicates that these have not been borrowed from Kullu, atleast not in their present form. There seems to be two reasons for this. Firstly, some people migrated from Kullu, particularly from Bara Bhangal which at that time was part of Kullu's territory. It is possible that these migrants might have composed the Ghures. Secondly when Lahaul was under the domain of the Raja of Kullu, the people of Lahaul had the responsibility of guarding the Raja's palace. Small group of people performed this duty. During the cold winter nights, they would make fire and sit around it the whole night. They enjoyed by singing Ghures with a view to pass the time. It is said that most of the Ghures were composed during that time. It is also possible that these migrants might have to sing the Ghures for the Raja, thus making it essential to compose them in the Kulluvi dialect.

Ghures are full of stories and information which needs to be preserved.

Pangwal Geet

The songs that accompany dance–music fall under this category. The language of these songs is mixed Hindustani. The name Pangwal Geet means the "Songs of Pangwal", suggesting that the origin of these songs might have been in Pangi in Chamba district. Perhaps the songs in earlier times might have been in Pangi dialect, but the present ones are certainly not in that dialect. Actually, the songs were preserved in an outside dialect, i.e. Hindustani and later people continued to compose new ones also in similar dialect to the extent of their knowledge of dialect. Most of these songs which are common now-a-days have been composed in the broken and distorted Hindustani.

The theme of these songs is either a typical event or an activity, but rarely one with any historical significance. One of the most popular subjects is love affair. There are some songs about good or the bad deeds but the majority are about bad deeds or immoral actions because pre-marital love affairs are not quite acceptable and any such incident quickly becomes a target for those who like to compose these songs.

In recent years popular movie songs are also taking the place of locally composed or traditional ones. Also a few songs composed in local dialects are becoming popular.

Sugili

The Sugili which is mostly composed as an eulogy, is sung at the time of funeral, although there are no restrictions on singing it at any time. At present Sugili are rarely heard. Most of the modern generation may never have heard of them. Occasionally Harijan women used to sing these songs when someone quite popular and respected dies.

Often they were composed and sung right on the spot by simply substituting the names in an existing Sugili. In some areas of Lahaul, Sugili is known as Surgin.

Historical Song

Many Historical Songs are sung in Lahaul and mostly these are Ghures, some common songs are:

Ghure

Sonam sikari e sikara taiyari
Sonam sikari e sikara taiyari
Sonam babu thalave lagi ho
Mat Janda putrara kunseri byali ho
Sonam sikari e mangeri nahi ho
Sonam mayie thalane lagi ho
Mat Janda putrara kunseri byali ho
Sonam sikariye manare ri tahi ho
Sonam ladiye thalane lagi ho
Mat Janda kwanda kunseri byali ho
Sonam sikariye manane ri nahi ho
Sonam sikariye sikara gaiya ho
Shanki kutari saiye chalori ho
Sonam sikariye sata surgani khaya
Shanki kutari e ghare jogu ayi ho
Sonam sikariye sikara taiyari ho

This song is sung without the accompaniment of any instrument. No Tala is played. It is sung in a very slow tempo and the words are elongated according to the execution by the singer.

Pa	pa	ma	ma	ma	re	sa	*ni*	pa
so	na	m	si	ka	a	ri	-i	he

sa	re	sa	ma	-	pa	mare	ma	-	re	-	sa	-
si	ka	ia	ka	a	ra	tai ya	a		ri	i	ho	o

ni	sa	re	ma	ma	ma	re	sa	ni	pa
so	o	na	m	si	ka	a	ri	i	he

sa	re	sa	ma	-	pa	ma	re	ma	-	re	-	sa	-
si	i	i	ka	a	ra	ta	ya	a	a	ri	i	ho	o

The whole song is sung in the same manner.

This song is known as *Ghure*. These are ritual songs which are sung on the occasion of some rituals or ceremonies. This particular song is sung on the occasion of *Kunh* during winter season. The description of Devils comes along with the description of Gods. It is also believed that during *Kunh* days the evil spirits and ghosts attack the persons. So everybody should be cautious of them. This song is a story of a hunter named Sonam who wants to go for hunting during the *Kunh* days. People forbid him but he is ready to go ignoring the advice of the elder people. Sonam says that he must go. The elder man says that it is not a good omen since the Gods will not come to save him due to the power of the devils during *Kunh* days. But Sonam is adament and he goes out to the forests for hunting. He was empowered by *Sat-surgini* (evil spirits) and was killed by them. The whole *Ghure* is the description of this episode.

Historical Ghure

Yunderi dhyari fagari jattre ji ho
Bhai chare bangle andre ji ho
Rami chand Nandiram gun gunande ji ho
Guni sunu gun gunanda ji ho
Vaman Shiv dayal hathe ri sudake ji ho
Rana Dunichand bangle andre ji ho
Chela Karamdas supna sunada ji ho
Tunderi thari vo hivani auni ji ho

Papi amra bura rudane lagi ji ho

Rati kara bele drana guti ayi ji ho

Tunderi sare hivane geye ji ho

Chela Karamdase haka hoka ditti ji ho

Dundreri loko jinde kimoye ji ho

Muti, Taji ram ri khabar nahi ji ho

Hori sare vo raji na baji ji ho

Each line is repeated twice.

The main theme of this song is about the forthcoming conditions of Lahaul. The elderly people sit together during the cold winter nights and sing this song. The *Gur Chela* recalls his dreams and forcasts some incidents which may happen. He tells that a great snow blizzard will occur. Avalanches may disturb the valley. His forcasts become true and whole of the Trilokinath village came under heavy snow. Muti and Sajiram, these two persons were killed in this storm. The only survival was Nand Ram. who was the eye witness of this mishappening. He recalls this incident to his friends. His eyes are full of tears while reciting this story.

This Ghure is particularly sung during the Kunh festival. Everyone feels sad to listen to the tragedy.

Notation (without accompaniment)

sa	*ni*	pa	*ni*	sa	re	re	re	ma	re	sa	*ni*
y	un	de	ri	i	dhya		a	ri	fa	a	ga	a

re	ma	pa	ma	re	sa	-	-	-	-	-
di	ja	a	a	tre	ji	ho	o	o	o	o	o

sa	ni	pa	ni	sa	re	re	re	ma	re	sa	ni
bha a	a	a	yi	cha a		re	ba	an	g	le

re	ma	pa	ma	re	ni	sa	-	-	-	-	-
an	d	a	a	re	ji	ho	-	o	o	o	o

The whole song is sung in the above mentioned tune. Each line is repeated twice.

Ghure-Historical song

Tindanu puhala he hinseri grave ji ho
Tindanu puhala he hinseri grave ji ho
Tindana puhala he bheda bakari chari ji ho
Bheda bakari vo niji murti re dhare ji ho
Niji murti vo dungeri gothe ji ho
Tindanu puhala he sukheya sutora ji ho
Sata murti he khel khilave ji ho
Sata murti he bheda bakari dudhe ji ho
Shankheri murti he shankhe damaru ji ho
Tindanu puhala he ghare jogu aya ji ho
Grave hinswale gari mawari dende ji ho
Tindanu puhala vo dudh dai peenda ji ho
Tindanu puhala vo gave saughandh karda ji ho
Eki roje vo chhupi kina baitha ji ho
Sata murti he dudha dune laggi ji ho
Eki murti he pakri na leyi ji ho
Jo var mangla teu seu var deula ji ho
Tindanu puhala vo manneri nahi ji ho
Saiyo murti ho hinse jo layi ji ho
Saiyo murti ho tunde jo layi ji ho
Mera namevo Trilokinatha ji ho
Mere agre vo ateel deeva ji ho
Tindanu puhala he

This song is related to the establishment of the deity of Triloknath. It is believed that nobody had installed the idol but it had itself emerged. A shepherd named Tindanu found it in the forest and brought it here. He installed the idol at Triloknath village . People asked him to give away that idol but the shepherd did not agree. Later, a splendid temple was erected at the place where the idol was installed.

This *Ghure* song is sung at the various ceremonies and festivals related to Triloknath. Ritual worship is performed before this *Ghure* is sung and it is also believed that this *Ghure* must be sung in full and should not be left hay-way.

Notation (without any accompaniment)

pa	ma	ma	re	sa	dh	sa	re	-
t	in	da	nu	pu	ha	a	la	a

sa	sa	re	ma	pa	ma	re	sa
he	hi	in	se	e	e	e	ri

dh	sa	re	ma	re	sa	sa	-
gra	a	a	ve	e	ji	ho	o

pa	ma	ma	re	sa	dh	sa	re	-
ti	in	da	nu	pu	u	ha	la	a

sa	sa	re	ma	pa	ma	re	sa
he	bhe	e	da	ba	a	ka	ri

dha	sa	re	ma	re	sa	sa	-
cha	a	a	ri	i	ji	ho	o

The whole song is sung in the same tune.

Enu seri granen gwadu pawalu rakhe ji o
Gwadu pawalu mainge ri dhare ji o

Lacha chari mainge ri dhare ji o
Mainge ri dhare niji moorti ase ji o
Niji murti sata murta nigati
Sata murta khela khelande ji o

This 'Ghure' is connected with the installation of the idol of Lord Trilokinath. Description about who brought the idol and how it was installed in the temple is given. It is believed that at Mainge Dhar around a spring there were seven idols and the idol which was installed in the temple of Trilok Nath is one of them. These lines are song as a part of the long song.

Notation Set to seven beat *Tala*

-	-	-	pa	ma	pama	re	Sa	dha	sa	resa	sa	sa	-
-	-	-	e	e	nu	se	ri	gra	a	ven	o	o	o
x			2		3	x	2			3			

sare	ma	re	ma	ma	re	sa	dhasa	re	ma	re	sa	sa	-
gwa	ru	u	pa	ma	lu	u	ra	a	aa	khe	e	ji	i
x			2		3		x			2		3	

Reset of the line are sung in the same tune. Each line is repeated twice.

Ghure, Rupi Rani

Mooran shuki kulh shuki
Pani nayi tee puje
Gunsheri panu nara shukara geyi je
Chambe ayi udetu roda
Rane ri praudi kadi je
Rane ri praudi kadi je
Poti pati ri heri je
Pati ri andoo raje
Kardi kutti bata je

Undo mama teetu mayita

Mana suba kiti je

This song is a narration of the sacrifice of Rupi Rani. Rupi Rani was the sister of the king of Chamba and was married to the king of Lahaul. There was severe drought and no water in the Ghushal village of Lahaul. People were much worried and panicky. Fortunately, a *Sadhu* happened to be there and he informed that the water can come to the village after a sacrifice and he suggested many options to give sacrifice. After the offering of sacrifice the water came to village Ghushal. The people of Lahaul sing this song in praise of Rupi Rani who sacrificed her life for the village. During winters Lahaulas sing this song for hours together. These are the opening lines of a very long story in verse.

Notation. Set to ten beats *Tala*.

1	2		3	4	5		6	7		8	9	10	
ma	mare		ma	pa	pama		pani	pama		mare	sasa	ni	
moo	ran		shu	ki	ii		ku	lh		shu	ki	i	
x			2				o			3			

sare	mama		re	sasa	ni		resa	rema		resa	sa	-	
pa	ni		na	ain	e		tee	e, ee		pu	je	e	
x			2				o			3			

Mythological Song

Krishna -   Sun sun mata Yashoda

Mau chhinja jana jarure

Sun sun mata Yashoda

Mau chhinja jana jarure

Yashoda-   Tu mera balak yana

Tau mere mari mukale

Krishna-   Hori joga dham padam

Kanejo likhi parwane

Yashoda-	Tu mera balak yana
	Tau mere mari mukale
Krishna-	Sun sun mata Yashoda
	Mau chhinja jana jarure
Yashoda-	Tu jana chhinja Kanaure
	Mau gada daud lagau
Krishna-	Tu gada daud lagali
	Mau jodi pahara lagau
Yashoda-	Tu jana chhinja Kanaure
	Mau nadi chhad bhareli
Krishna-	Tu nadi chhal mareli
	Mau jodi tarn lagau
Krishna-	Sun sun mata Yashoda
Krishna-	Mau chhake keera lagore
Yashoda-	Kanauri peta o chou
	Khund prithvi basori
Krishna-	Sun sun mata Yashoda
	Mau chhinja jana jarure
Yashoda-	Tu mera balak yana
	Tau mere mari mukale
	Tu mera balak yana
	Tau mere mari mukale

Notation- *Tala Dadra* (fast)

Dhadha	dhani	pama		re-	re-	ma-
sun	su	n		ma	ta	ja
ma	re	sa		sare	sani	nisa
so	o	da		mau	chnin	ja
rema	mare	nisa		sa	ni	pa
jaa	na	ja		ru	u	re
Dha	dha	sani		ni	pa	pa
su	n	su		n	ma	a

sa-	re	ma		ma	re	sa-
ta	ya	a		sho	o	da

This song is sung during "Kunh", festival. This is an episode depicting the bravery of Lord Krishna. Krishna has been challenged for wrestling by Kans. He asks the permission of Yashoda to go for the wrestling bout but she is afraid that Krishna is so young and how will he fight with Kans. Krishna assures her that he will come back after killing Kans. Yashoda blesses Krishna and prays for his success.

The people make merry during 'Kunh' festival. They dance along with the beat of this song. The dance is a group dance. People put on their traditional dresses. They dance enthusiastically with swaying footwork and thus celebrate the festival singing the victory of Lord Krishna over Kans.

Mythological Song

Jab dhiye raja pandaru
Tab thiye nau gaj mahnu ho
Jab dhiye raja pandaru
Tab thiye sat gaj janana ho
Jab dhiye raja pandaru
Tab thiye ghoriyere dudha ho
Jab dhiye raja pandaru
Tab thiye ghorire seenga ho
Jab dhiye raja pandaru
Tab thiye ser anaja ho
Jab dhiye raja pandaru
Tab thiye kakul jooan ho
Jab dhiye raja pandaru
Tab thiye nau gaj mahnu ho
Jab dhiye raja pandaru
Tab thiye ser anaja ho

Notation *Tala Kehrawa*

pa	ni	sa	sa		ni	-	re	-
ja	b	dhi	i		ye	e	ra	a
x					o			
pa	-	ma	re		sa	ni	pa	-
ya	a	pa	an		da	a	ru	u
pa	ni	re	-		-	ma	re	sa
ta	b	dhi	i		i	ye	na	u
x					o			
pa	ni	sa	sa		sa	ni	pa	-
ga	ja	ma	ah		nu	u	ho	o
x					o			
pa	ni	sa	sa		ni	-	re	-
ya	b	dhi	i		ye	e	ra	a
x					o			
pa	-	ma	re		sa	ni	pa	-
ya	a	pa	an		da	a	ru	u
x					o			
pa	ni	re	-		-	ma	re	sa
ta	b	dhi	i		i	ye	se	r
x					o			
pa	ni	sa	sa		sa	ni	pa	-
a	a	na	a		ja	a	ho	o
x					o			

The whole song is sung in the same manner.

It is a mythological song that describes the kingdom and state of the world during the period of the *Pandavas*. At that time everything was different from these days, human-beings as well as the animals were different. The man used to be as tall as nine yards and women seven yards. A seed of the grain used to be one seer (equal to 954 gm). The birds were different. The horses had horns and the birds used to give milk. Very strange things used to exist as compared to these days. Such was the time when the Pandavas used to rule the country.

SONGS RELATED TO CEREMONIES FAIRS AND FESTIVALS

Wedding Songs.

Mameri khoka bhaneji roladi
Mameri khoka bhaneji roladi
Role mate bhaneji twaja na deule
Role mate bhaneji twaja na deule
Twaja na mama bari puji geya
Twaja na mama bari puji geya
Bhau jogu lodi megeri bare
Bhau jogu lodi megeri bare
Thoda na lodi bahuta lodi
Thoda na lodi bahuta lodi
Gaure e deyi khine khine hasadi
Gaura e deyi khine khine hasadi
Kiyan ayila kodi diye biyahe le la
Kiyan ayila kodi diye biyahe lela

Notation *Tala Dadra* (fast)

sani	pani	sa-	|	-	ga	maga
ma	me	ri	|	-	kho	ka
x			|	o		
sani	nini	ni-	|	sa	ga	ga
bha	he	ji	|	ro	la	di
gama	ga	sa	|	pani	sa	ga
ma	me	ri	|	kho	ka	a
x			|	o		
maga	gama	ma	|	ma	ga	sa
bha	ne	ji	|	ro	la	di
x			|	o		

Rest of the song is sung in the same tune. Each line is repeated twice.

It is called "Byahonda" meaning a wedding song. It is sung in the brides side. This song is sung during the marriage ceremony, when the girl is being prepared for the marriage ceremony and she is given a bath.

It is a song depicting the feelings of a bride. It is the desire of every bride to get a handsome husband. The bride requests her parents that she should not be married to an ugly person. She compares herself to Parvati and her husband to Lord Shiva. She says that she does not want to get married to a person who seems like a leper. She cries and asks her maternal uncle to save her from such a marriage. Her uncle says that she will be given many ornaments, jewellery and all beautiful things so she should not cry and get ready for the marriage.

She says that she has already received so many things and there is no dearth of things for her but she requests to save her from this ugly person who has come to marry her.

O, God, please give plenty of snow. I request you to shower so much snow that all the lofty hill-tops and high mountains may be covered with snow and the traffic may be blocked so that he is not able to reach here to marry me.

Wedding Song (Vidayi Geet)

La diva la paira mochadi
La tau jana pardesha he
La diva la paira mochadi
La tau jana pardeshe he
La diva la hatha kanganu

La tau jana pardesha he
La diva la hatha kanganu
La tau jana pardesha he
La diva la peedhi lodusu
La tau jana pardesha he
La diva la peedhi lodusu
La tau jana pardesha he

Notation *Tala - Dadra* (fast)

saga	sani	saga		madha	maga	maga
La	diva	la		paira	mo	chadi
sa	-	-		saga	maga	sani
La	a	a		tau	ja	na
x				o		
dhadha	dhani	saga		sa	-	-
par	de	sha		he	e	e
x				o		

This song is sung at the time of departure of the bride to her in-law's house.

The bride is dressed up and she is asked to adore herself with new clothes, jewellery, shoes and other bridal make-up. The girl is addressed as "*Diva*". She is advised to get ready to go to her in-laws. So she should be dressed up beautifully.

The tune of this song is very pathetic. The feeling of leaving the parent's house is very touching and it is very well expressed through this song. The stmosphere is so touchy and sad that everybody present at the time of departure of the bride begins to weep as if their own dear daughter is parting away.

This song is a wedding song. When the bridegroom is leaving towards the bride's place for the marriage ceremony, this

song is sung by the leader of the bridegroom's party. The leader
is called the *Shirdaar*.

Wedding Song

Raja e Rama Lanka jo varde
Rishi muni jogu dhame vo
Raja e Rama Lanka jo varde
Nau lakh tare jo dhame vo
Rana e Rama Lanka jo varde
Sooraj chandre jo dhame vo
Raja e Rama Lanka jo varde
Sunku veera jo dhame vo
Raja e Rama Lanka jo varde
Dharati mata jo dhame vo
Raja e Rama Lanka jo varde
Chaukhund prithvi jo dhame vo

Notation *Tala Dadra*

re	re	sa	re	ma	pa	ma	ma	re	sa	ni	pa
ra	ja	e	ra	a	ma	lan	ka	jo	va	r	de
x			o			x			o		
pa	ma	re	ni	sa	re	sa	sa	sa	ni	pa	pa
ri	shi	mu	hi	i	jo	gu	dha a		me	vo	o
x			o			x			o		
re	re	sa	re	ma	pa	ma	ma	re	sa	ni	pa
ra	ja	e	ra	a	ma	lan	ka	jo	va	r	de
x			o			x			o		
pa	ma	re	ni	sa	re	sa	sa	sa	sa	ni	pa
nau la		kh	ta	a	re	jo	dha a		me	vo	o
x			o			x			o		

The whole song is sung in the same tune. Each line is
repeated twice every time.

The song has the description of the episode when Lord Rama was going to attack Lanka to bring back Sita from the captivity of Ravana. To join Rama in this attack, invitations were sent to all the warriors and brave-men. The earth, nine lakh stars, the sun, the moon and every-one was invited to join the army of Lord Rama to attack Lanka so that Sita could be saved from the jail of Ravana.

Through this song the message of bravery of Rama and his love for Sita has been conveyed. In Lahaul, every bride is compared to Sita and the bridegroom to Rama. Different episodes are sung from the Ramayana on the occasion of marriage ceremony.

Pauri Festival Song

Bhayaji revak pauri jana gamade
Bhayaji revak pauri jana gamade
Bhayaji dhurap ka padra dera gamade
Bhayaji dhurap ka padra dera gamade
Bhayaji Thirota padra dera gamade
Bhayaji Thirota padra dera gamade
Bhayaji Tunde vayadi sela gamade
Bhayaji Tunde vayadi sela gamade
Bhayaji mane koro dena gamade
Bhayaji mane koro dena gamade
Bhayaji sata koro dena gamade
Bhayaji sata koro dena gamade
Bhayaji gheeve chhoname kiye gamade
Bhayaji gheeve chhoname kiye gamade

Another version of this song goes like the following one:-

Bayaji Devna pauri jana nasha le
Bayaji Devna pauri jana nasha le
Bayaji Chhesu gompa jana nasha le
Bayaji Chhesu gompa jana nasha le
Bayaji kya hala hoi nasha le
Bayaji kya hala hoi nasha le
Bayaji babu gala suni nasha le
Bayaji babu gala suni nasha le
Baya ji kishmat khota hoi nasha le
Baya ji kishmat khota hoi nasha le
Bayaji babu gala baithi nashale
Bayaji babu gala baithi nashale
Bayaji hun Tala kothi jana nasha le
Bayaji hun Tala kothi jana nasha le
Bayaji Kardung gompa jana nasha le
Bayaji Kardung gompa jana nasha le
Bayaji pyokari gala baithi nasha le
Bayaji pyokari gala baithi nasha le
Bayaji jang janga kothi jana nasha le
Bayaji jang janga kothi jana nasha le
Bayaji Devna pauri jana nasha le
Bayaji Devna pauri jana nasha le

I would like to go to Pauri festival, which is being celebrated in the village of Triloknath. On the way there are many religious places and I will offer my obeisance there. I would like to go to Devna Pauri, Chheshu Gompa and Kardang Gompa to pay my homage to the deities.

Notation *Tala Dadra*

Sa	re	ga		ga	re	-		ga	ma	ga		ga	ma	ga
De	va	na		pau	ri	i		ja	na	a		na	sha	a
x				o										

```
sa  -   -   |  ga  ma  ga  |  re  dha  -  |  -  -  -
le  e   e   |  ba  ya  a   |  ji  i    i  |  -  -  -
x           |  o
```

Each line is repeated twice. The whole song is sung in the same manner.

Social Theme Songs

Some of the Common Folk songs related to social themes are:

Ek din mari jana sagala sensara chhodi jana ho
Ek din mari jana sagala sansara chhodi jana ho
Ek din mari jana mayi babu chhodi jana ho
Ek din mari jana grayin gotha chhodi jana ho
Ek din mari jana jimi bhumi chhodi jana ho
Ek din mari jana, bhai bahin chhodi jana ho
Ek din mari jana dhayi gaj kapada leyi jana ho
Ek din mari jana sagala sansara chhodi jana ho

Notation *Tala Kehrawa* (fast)

```
sa   re   mare   ma   |  sa      -    ni   -
e    k    di     n    |  ma      a    ri   i
x    |    o
ni   -    pa     -    |  re      re   re   ma
ja   a    na     a    |  sa      ga   l    sen
x                     |  x
pa   -    ma     re   |  sa      -    ni   -
sa   a    ra     a    |  chho    o    di   i
x                     |  x
pa   ni   re     -    |  sa      -    -    -
ja   a    na     a    |  ho      o    o    o
x                     |  x
```

sa	re	mare	ma		sa	-	ni	-
e	k	di	n		ma	a	ri	i
x					x			
ni	-	pa	-		re	re	re	ma
ja	a	ha	a		ma	a	yi	i
x					x			
pa	-	ma	re		sa	-	ni	-
ba	a	bu	u		chho	o	di	i
x					x			
pa	ni	re	-		sa	-	-	-
ja	a	na	a		ho	o	o	o
x					x.			

The whole song is sung in the same tune.

The song describes the mortality characteristics of human beings. Since man is mortal he should do good to others during his life-time. Man has to leave everything at the time of death. Nothing goes with him. After death there is no relation and attachment to worldly things. So he must always remember that he has to die one day and will leave the world. It is his duty to do good to others so that people may remember him even after his death.

Another Social Theme song

Na jure bhai na jure toota sheesha na jure
Na jure bhai na jure toota sheesha na jure
Na jureh bhai na jure dile dara na jure
Na jureh bhai na jure dile dara na jure
Na jure bhai na jure aisi yari na jure
Na jure bhai na jure aisi yari na jure
Na jure bhai na jure prema pyari na jure
Na jure bhai na jure prema pyari na jure

Na jure bhai na jure yari dosta na jure

Na jure bhai na jure yari dosta na jure

The main theme of this song is that a broken thing can not be repaired and brought in its original form. For example, if a glass is broken it cannot be brought back in its original shape and if a thread breaks, it requires a knot to join it, and, the knot is clearly visible. So, one should remain friendly with others and should not do any such work for which he has to repent afterwards.

Notation *Tala Kehrawa* (fast)

sare	-ma	mare	sadha		sare	-ma	ma	-pa
na	aju	reh	bhai		na	aju	reh	ee
x					x			
dhapa	mare	mare	sadha		sare	resa	sa	-
too	ta	sec	sa		na	aju	reh	e
x					x			

Social Theme Song

Moti lala aisa mehfil kadon milana

Moti lala aisa mehfil kadon milana

Moti lala diledar kadon milana

Moti lala diledar kadon milana

Moti lala bhai babu kadon milane

Moti lala bhai babu kadon milane

Moti lala aisa dost kadon milana

Moti lala aisa dost kadon milana

Moti lala bhai bhraon kadon milana

Moti lala bhai bhraon kadon milana

Moti lala songa sogi kadon milane

Moti lala songa sogi kadon milane.

This song is sung in praise of Lala Motilal who has been snatched away through the cruel hands of death. Moti Lal was a very kind person and the people of Lahaul still remember him and they believe that they will never find a friend like Motilal. He was very gentle, co-operative and kind person. He was like a brother and a good friend. Motilal always behaved like an elder person, We can never find a person like Motilal.

Social Theme song

Bhava mat janda kanwar desha ho
Bhava mat janda kanwar desha ho
Bhava kanwar Suliyar rani ho
Bhava kanwar Suliyar rani ho
Bhava Suliyar jadu karandi ho
Bhava Suliyar jadu karandi ho
Bhava deena vo bhedu banaudi ho
Bhava deena vo bhedu banandi ho
Bhava rati vo khasam banandi ho
Bhava rati vo khasam banandi ho
Bhava mat janda kanwar desha ho
Bhava mat janda kanwar desha ho

A sister warns her brother that he should not go to the *Kanwar* country. *Kanwar* is referred to the Kamrup, the Assam of to-day. Rani Suliyar resided there. She knew the art of magic and with this power of magic she could turn a man into a sheep during the day time but turned him into a man and then treat him as her husband during the night. So you should be careful and should not go to the *Kanwar* county.

LOVE SONGS

Angmo's Song

> Jis pe Angmo pardesi sanga
> Angmo mera chala ni jana o
> Jis pe Angmo sharam bigadi
> Angmo mera chala ni jana o
> Jis pe Angmo des chhodi jana
> Angmo mera chala ni jana o
> Jis pe Angmo kis kisa bana
> Angmo mera chala ni jana o
> Jis pe Angmo nava faishon bana
> Angmo mera chala ni jana o

This is a love song. Angmo is the heroine of this song. The hero says that he does not want to go with a damsel who is not of good character and she has brought shame for the family by doing unwanted acts. The hero warns Angmo that she should not do such acts which may malafide the name of the family. The whole song has a list of unwanted deeds which should be avoided.

Notation: *Tala Dadra* (fast)

sa	sasa	-		re	gapa	-
ji	spe	e		an	gmo	o
x				x		
pa	dhapa-	pa		pare	gare	-
pa	rde	esi		san	aga	a
x				x		
ga	dhapa	m		g	asa	
a	gamo	o		gare	gasa	-
x				x		

rega	gare	sani		pa	dhasa	-
cha	la	ni		ja	ana	a
x	-	-		-	-	-
sa	-	-		-	-	-
o	o	o		o	o	o
x				x		

Semo Gappa Song

Semo gappa sairig ho hengu jaodi banekti ho
Semo gappa sairig ho hendu jodi bahekti ho
Ya ba maruktishi ho hengu banekti ho
Ya ba maruktishi ho hengu banekti ho
Teere teere khanshi ho hengu jodi banekti ho
Teere teere khanshi ho hengu jodi banekti ho
Dane bajara sela ho henge hodi banekti ho
Dane bajara sela ho henge hodi banekti ho
Bhatte geeje khadare ho liengu jodi banekti ho
Bhatte geeje khadare ho liengu jodi banekti ho

This song is sung during the weddings by young boys and girls. It tells that both the boy and the girl are married as they have been united by the wedlock. They are made for each other and nobody can separate them. God has made them for each other.

DEVELOPMENT SONG

Bijli ra kama ho chhota Shansha chamka ho -
Shansha kirting lighta ho
Chhota Shansha chamka ho
Chhota Shansha chamka ho
Ghare ghare khushi ho chhota Shausha chamka ho
Kirting nada kaam ho chhota Shausha chamka ho
Jage jage lighta ho chhota Shansha chamka ho
Pani pawar housa ho chhota Shausha chamka ho

The description of the developmental activities going on in Lahaul are given in this song. It is said that the Chhota Shansha (name of the place in Lahaul) is illuminating since the electricity has reached there. Every-one is feeling happy. The power- house has been established in Chhota Shansha. People are happy all over Keylong. The people are grateful to the government who is doing such developmental activities.

Notation *Tala Kehrawa* (fast)

ga	pa	pa	ga	ga	re	sa	re	ga	pa	re	ga	re	-	-	-
pa	a	wa	r	hau	au	sa	a	ka	a	a	ma	o	o	o	o
x				x				x				x			
sa	re	re	ga	pa	ga	re	-	re	sa	re	as	sa	-	-	-
chho	o	ta	a	shan	a	sa	a	cha	a	ma	ka	o	o	o	o
x				x				x				x			

The whole of the song is sung in the same tune.

POLITICAL SONG

Sthai

Swagla desh hendu ruthe ho sadhire
Swagla desh hendu ruthe ho sadhire

Antra

Changsa, Losa, Gahari, Totapa
Icho nado pyar henar shui ho sadhire
Swagla desh.............
Hendu gude rahansi pachhansi
Hendu gude poga pahansi
Banejar be ruthe hendu poga ho sadhire
Swagla desh.............

This song is in the praise of Lahaul where people of all the areas of Lahaul live peacefully and co-operate with each other, though there is so much diversity among the different valleys of Lahaul. Moreover, people observe different religious rituals as they follow different religions. All the residents of all valleys of the Lahaul live unitedly, and they do hard work and the artifects are unique.

This song is usually sung to the accompaniment of dance.

Notation *Tala Kehrawa* (fast)

Sthai

sa	re	ma	pa		dha	pama	pa	rere
swa	g	la	a		de	esh	hen	du
x					2			
re	ma	-	pa		mare	re-	sa	-
ru	the	e	ho		sa	di	re	e
x					2			

Antra

dha	sa	sa	sa		sa	re	sa	dha
cha	g	sa	a		lo	o	sa	a
x					2			
pa	dha	pa	ma		mapa	mapa	dha	-
ga	ha	ri	i		to	ta	pa	a
x					2			
sa	re	ma	pa		dha	pama	pa	rere
i	cho	na	ho		pya	ar	he	nar
x					2			
re	ma	-	pa		mare	re-	sa	-
shu	yi	i	ho		sa	di	re	e
x					2			

Tashi Kalzam's song

Pare bane o eki miruge ase o -
Pare bane o eki miruge ase o -

Putra Tashi Kalzam hede jo tyari o -
Putra Tashi Kalzam hede jo tyari o -
Mai tan babue samujhane lagi o -
Mai tan babue samujhane lagi o -
Putra Tashi Kalzam manune ri nai o-
Putra Tashi Kalzam manune ri nai o-
Ladi tan Zila Zom samujhane lagi o -
Ladi tan Zila Zom samujhane lagi o -
Putra Tashi Kalzam manune ri nai o-
Putra Tashi Kalzam manune ri nai o-
Pare bane o gaja gaja hinve o
Pare bane o gaja gaja hinve o
Putra Tashi Kalzam banduka swari o -
Putra Tashi Kalzam banduka swari o -
Putra Tashi Kalzam bauduka bhari o-
Putra Tashi Kalzam bauduka bhari o-

This song is a story of Tashi Kalzam who was a brave man and wanted to go for hunting. Tashi Kalzam was ready to go for hunting but his mother and father forbade him to go to the forest because it was inhabited by fierce "*Bagh (leopard)*" who had become maneater. But Tashi Kalzam insisted on going. His wife Zila Zom forbade Tashi Kalzam. She said that in those forests there is lot of snow and every-thing is under the thick layer of snow. There are also your enemies who have come here with their loaded guns. They will kill you. So I pray that you should not go for hunting but Tashi Kalzam did not listen to them and went to the forest. It is believed that he was killed by the furocious leopard.

Notation Set to *Tala* of seven beats

-	-	-		dha	-		sa	sa		ga	re	-		ga	pa		ga	pa
-	-	-		pa	a		re	e		ba	a	a		ne	e		o	o
x				2			3			x				2			3	

ga	ga	re		re	dha		sa	-		rega sa	-		sa	-		-	-
e	ki	i		mi	ru		ge	e		aa	a	a	se	e		e	e
x				2			3			x			2			3	
re	ga	re		re	resa		dha	sa		pa	dha	-	pa	-		-	-
o	o	o		e	pa		re	e		ba	a	a	he	e		e	e
x				2			3			x			2			3	
dha	sa	dha		pa	ga		pa	-		dha	sa	-	sa	-		-	-
e	ki	i		mi	ru		ge	e		a	a	a	se	e		e	e
x				2			3			x			2			3	

PATRIOTIC SONG

Desho naujawan desha keno shunde
Desha keno yori evi dharau sadhire
Desho desha dhava deeye desho shunde
Jushi ati sehta duta ramoyi sadhire
Desho raksha laji hendu farz shunde
Jushi ati sehta dula ramoyi sadhire
Desho naujawan desha deno shunde
Desha keno yori evi dharau sadhire

This patriotic song is accompanied with a dance of fast tempo. Young boys and girls participate in the dance artistically.

The main theme of this song is that whatever wealth and treasure is owned by Lahaul, is of the country. As such every person of Lahaul, is of the country. As such every person of Lahaul is ready to sacrifice every thing for the sake of the beloved country. Whenever the country is in need of any type of sacrifice, the people of Lahaul will sacrifice it happily. To save the country is prestige of the people of Lahaul who are ever ready to sacrifice their wealth, property and even their lives. May the country live long.

Notation *Tala Kehrawa* (fast)

sadha	padha	sarega	pa-		padha	pama	garesa	re-
de	sho	nauja	wan		desh	keno	shun	de
x					x			
rega	papa	gare	sa-		rega	resadha	padha	sa-
desh	deho	yo	ri		ivi	dharau	sa	di
x					x			
sa-	sadha	sare	gare		-	-	-	-
re	he	ee	ee		-	-	-	-
x								

Patriotic Song

Sthai

Bhai saheb ji Keylong sela
Bhai saheb ji Keylong sela

Antra

Keylong hendu rajdhani
Keylong hendu rajdhani
Bhai saheb ji Keylong sela
Bhai saheb ji Keylong sela
Ti tungami nalaka tamasha saleema ji
Ti tungami nalaka tamasha saleema ji
Bhai saheb ji Keylong sela
Bhai saheb ji Keylong sela
Adu ta Uptodate Rashan Miskan ji
Adu ta Uptodate Rashan Miskan ji
Bhai saheb ji Keylong sela.
Bhai saheb ji Keylong sela.
Keylong kothi rangi rangi
Keylong kothi rangi rangi
Bhai saheb ji Keylong sela.
Bhai saheb ji Keylong sela.

Keylong bijli jhili mili ji lo
Keylong bijli jhili mili ji lo
Bhai saheb ji Keylong sela
Bhai saheb ji Keylong sela

This song is accompanied by a dance of fast tempo. It is also sung on the occasion of political and social celebrations or on national days. The young boys and girls participate in this dance with great enthusiasm.

This song is sung in the praise of Keylong which is the headquarters of Lahaul district.

The main theme of the song is that Keylong is the most beautiful and attractive place of Lahaul valley. There are big buildings, natural scenic beauty spots and Keylong is illuminaing due to electricity. Such is the beauty of Keylong. Let us take all of you to visit Keylong and appreciate its natural beauty.

Notation *Tala Kehrawa* (fast)
Sthai

sasa	garesa	re-	-		sarega	sa	sasa	dha
bhai	saheb	ji	ii		keylo	ong	se	la
x					x			

Antra

papapa	dha	sadha	pa		dhapa	gare	sa	saresadha
keylon	ag	he	tu		raj	dha	ni	ii
x					x			
sasa	gare	sa	re-		sarega	sa	sasa	dha
bhai	saheb	ji	i		kaylon	ag	se	la
x					2			
papa	dha	sadha	pa		dhapa	rega	dhapa	garesa
leetun	gami	nal	ka		tama	sha	sali	maji
x					x			

sasa	garesa re-	-	sarega	sa	sasa	dha
bhai	saheb ji	i	kaylon	ag	se	la
x			x			

Patriotic Song

Gatu ching giyu desh hola ho
Giyu sem leti Swangla ho - 2
Adu Chandramukhi jindgani hola ho
Giyu sem leti Swangla ho - 2
Shenu arhi rarha singi lapche hola ho
Giyu sem leti Swangla ho -2
Rangi rangi gore mukcha chokti hola ho
Giyu sem leti Swangla ho -2
Gotu vichang giyu desh hola ho
Giyu sem leti Swangla ho -2

This song is sung in the praise of the valley of the Lahaul. Lahaul is very dear to all of us. This valley is situated amongst high mountains. Agriculture is the main occupation of the valley. Potato is the cash crop of Lahaul valley. The high mountain-tops are covered with thick layers of white snow. Such is the land of the Lahaul, of which we are proud.

Notation *Tala Kehrawa*

pa pa	nipa	ma	ga	sa-	ma	ma	ma	ma	-	ga	sa	-	sa-	ma
-go o	tu	chini	g	giyu	de˙	e	sha	ho	o	la	ho	o	giyuse	
x			o			x					o			
-	ga	maga sa	ni	pa	sa	sa	ma	ma	ma ma		-	-	-	-
-	ma	le e	ti	i	swan	ga	la	a	ho o		-	-	-	-
x			o			x					o			

Patrotic song

Sthal

> He,e swaglota dharati ho
> Devata tu desha shu
> Devata tu desha shu

Antara

> Netingta pyare hendu tan desha
> Netingta pyare hendu tan desha
> Dharati hendu swarga shu
> Dharati hendu swarga shu
> He swaglota dharati ho
> Rang chokti Totpa lassi Vyasa rishi
> Rang chokti Totpa lassi Vyasa rishi
> Rishi muniu derashu
> Rishi muniu derashu
> He,e swaglota dharti ho
> Go Tokti Kailash Gojong Triloknath
> Go Tokti Kailash Gojong Triloknath
> Jalavi ta evee ho
> Jalavi ta evee ho
> He , e, swaglota dharati ho

This is another patriotic song sung in the praise of the valley of Lahaul. We love our valley of Lahaul more than our lives. This valley is the abode of Gods. The saints have come here for meditation and seek salvation. Lahaul is the land of gods, we regard and respect the valley of Lahaul.

Following is another patriotic song of Lahaul area related to the passing away of Sh Lal Bahadur Shastri, the then Prime Minister of India who died in Tashkent (Russia) while negotiating the end of Indo-Pak war.

Kho gaya bhai kho gaya

Pyara neta kho gaya

Tashkand meeting ho pyara neta kho gaya

Tashkand meeting ho pyara neta kho gaya

Dil dukhi hoya ho, pyara neta kho gaya

Dil dukhi hoya ho, pyara neta kho gaya

Desha chhodi gaya ho, pyara neta kho gaya

Desha chhodi gaya ho, pyara neta kho gaya

Khogya bhai kho gaya dildara kho gaya

Lal Bahadur Shastri, pyara neta kho gaya

Lal Bahadur Shastri, pyara neta kho gaya

This song was common after the death of Sh Lal Bahadur Shastri, who lost his life while serving the country. He had gone to Tashkent to attend a meeting. People express their sorrow on the sad demise of Lal Bahadur Shastri who had left our country.

LOK RAMAYANA SONG

This song describes the passing of a golden deer through the forest and Sita is eager to get that golden deer. She requests Rama to get that and as such Rama goes after the deer to catch him. Rama and Lakshaman were two handsome brothers. After the departure of Rama to the forests, Lakshman is forced to follow him by Sita.

Rama o Lachhumana duye sonduru bhai

Rama o Lachhumana baruye mangai

Seeta o rani baruye mangai

Triji barushe byahe bati ani

Naga loka gaiye nou nagini lagay.

Surga loka gaiye Surja Chandura logay

Adamma puri behra banaye

Adamma puri behra banaye

Adamma puri noulakha baage
Rama o Seeta pasa khelande
Rameri pasa sumulla baithi,
Seete-ri pasa kumulla baithi
Teere nu baate Seeteri nazure
Sona singa harani noulakha baage
Oomulla booti soomulla keeti,
Soomulla booti oomulla keeti
Peto peto Rama taindune pasa
Rama o beera bana sumoori
Agai agai douri sona singa harani,
Tetha peechhe douri Rama o beera
Adu na baate sochunde laagi
Adu na baate phiri kairi ayi
Doodheri katoru baati charai
Doodheri katoru rakuta bhari,
Tanbhayo Lachumana Rameripaike
Gheewe sanjoti baati charai
Gheewe sanjoti ishunde lagi,
Tan bhayo Lachhumana Rameri paike
Peepuleri patura aadi charai
Peepuleri putura shookunde lagi,
Tan bhayo Lachhumana Rameri paike

SONG OF SHIVA AND PARVATI

This an episode from the life of Lord Shiva and Parvati. After their marriage Parvati went to his parents house on some pretext. Her parents were not happy on her arrival as she has come after having a quarrel with Lord Shiva.

Manyi jamela poota je, bapu jamela dheewa je
Manyi jamela poota je, badhayi lagi je
Badhayi lagi e, nawana rakhi je

Bapu e jamela dheewa je badhayi lagi je

Badhayi lagie ravana rakhi je

Ishura beera e Gourani baru mangai je

Aitware bare o Gourani baru mangi je

Somare bare o byah othu keeti je

Ishura beera Gaurani saithe byahi je

Ishura Gauri e rani jhagura keeti je

Gouri na rani e pyouke nu douri je

Chandura mukha keri re Gauri je

Drui Raja Rameri bole je

Gouri na rani e rushi pyouke nu douri je

Adhuna manju bate jambu mata meri je

Jambu na mata e poochhune lagi je

Gouri na rani e kiji kame douri je

Gouri na rani Ishura saite jhagura keeti je

Gouri re pyouke o anukara geyi je

Asanti aye teehara nukuru grasa keeye deunle.

SONG OF THE RANAS OF GHUSHAL AND A GURA FROM WARI

This song has the description of the historical event of the war between Rana of Ghushal and a *Gura* from Wari in which Rana was victorious,

Bola chanani na lagi o, rimiyan na jhimiyan,

Suruga bharoru tarey;

Bola Ghooshe na lagi o, joguni re jaatrey,

Gure ri gaiye paikey;

Bola aukhi na dhruye deeti, Birubala rana,

Choura ditiru boley;

Bola jori na manu, wari jogu bhejey,

Trashi Prashi re poochhey;

Bola Trashi Parashi bola bolande

Nandi putra mere pyarey

Bola ageya chalundey, dhrageya nishani,
Peechhe chalande Nandi;
Bola pawa khelande Rokuru na Deburu,
Dera khelande Nandi;
Bola bhali kari nacha o Ghusheri gabhuru,
Patuka pyari teri douley;
Bola bhali kari nacha o Ghusheri gharani,
Moonga moti ghare ayey;
Bola bhali kari nacha o Ghusheri ani,
Enani munari teri vatey.

SONG OF RUPI RANI

It is a song describing the sacrifice of Rani Rupi who was instrumental in bringing water for the Kothi (village), Rani Rupi belonged to Chamba and was sad as the people did not have water for their daily needs, A *Jogi* (saint) came and put forward three solutions for the arrival of water to the village. It included the sacrifice of any of the three viz. black cat, black bitch or a member of the royal family. Rani Rupi did not allow the sacrifice of black cat or black bitch but she sacrificed herself for this cause. Similar event has also been reported from the Chamba region of Himachal Pradesh.

Oorana shooki moorana shooki pani nahi teepu je.
Ghunsheri panugana shookara geye je.
Udho mama Teetu Maita manasuba keeti je,
Chambe ayi Udetu roura Raneri prouri khari je,
Raneri prouri khari je pothi patiri heri je,
Patiri andura je kali kutti bata je.
Udho Mama Teetu Maita manashuba keeti je,
Kali kutti bata deunle, dwara koonu pahre la,
Patiri andura je kali bhiliri bata je,
Udho Mama Teetu Maita manasuba keeti je,

Kali bhiliri bata deunle chuli koonu pahre la
Patiri andura je ghunguru teeka bata je,
Idho Mama Teetu Maita manasuba keeti je,
Ghunguru teeka bata deunle rasi koonu sahme la;
Patiri andura je ghoonguru deyi bata je.
Udho Mama Teetu Maita manasuba keeti je,
Ghoonguru Deyi bata deunle Chamba kunu byahe la;
Patiri andura je Rupi Rani bata je.
Udho Mama Teetu Maita manasuba keeti je,
Hori dabo pyouke Ghusharu choochu matu dabe la,
Ghunguru Teeka ayela choochu to peeye la.
Hori dabo pyouke Ghusharu teera matu dabe la,
Ghoonguru Deyi ayela doomadu herey la.

SONG ABOUT SUN, MOON AND RAHU

It is a mythological song describing the evolution of earth and other planets. In this episode, the evolution of Sun, Moon and Rahu has been described in a similar manner as is believed.

Dharti mata e triye koori jami ji o,
Dharti mata e triye koori jami ji o,
Jetha jetha kuriye namu Naraina byahi ji o,
Tethi kana kuriye panja panduba byahi ji o,
Tethi kana kuriye lacha charune gaiye ji o,
Raghu domey o chori kari naina ji o.
Surja Chadura e aire nu gaiye ji o,
Aire nu gaiye o mirga su mari ji o,
Mirga mari e chuli chouka deeti ji o,
Chuli chouka deeti o rasoni swari ji o,
Rasoni swari e rasoni khayi ji o,
Rasoni khayi o trishuna lagi ji o,
Surja Chandura e pani topunde gaiye ji o,
Bune prehnare o khadura pani ji o,

Upuru prehnare o neembula pani ji o,
Eura prehnare o eka istiri aasay ji o,
Surja Chandura e poochhuni lagi ji o.
Bolo isutiri kunu teri mata ji o,
Bolo isutiri kunu tere pita ji o,
Bateri mahnu e kya e projana lagi ji o,
Bateri mahnu e bate jogu ghate ji o,
Surja Chandura e ghiri phiri pochhunde ji o,
Kunu tere mata e, kunu tere pita ji o,
Dharti mata e maindune mata ji o,
Vishnu bharari maindune pita ji o,
Surja Chandura e muhe muh hairi ji o,
Raghu re ghare o kya e kama kare la ji o,
Nawe teri lachhuna e nawe teri trishuna ji o,
Surja Chandura e poochhune lagi ji o,
Raghu re ghare o kya e kama kare la ji o,
Shiburata kooti e manda pakayi ji o,
Chandura bhai e apuni bouri cheeri ji o,
Bouri cheeri o bheni chhupayi ji o,

SONG ABOUT THE ESTABLISHMENT OF TRILOKNATH TEMPLE

This is an episode regarding the establishment of temple of Triloknath in Lahaul. A shepherd saw seven idols and was asked by one of the idol to take it to the village and then establish the temple. The episode goes on to describe the way as to how the shepherd saw and brought the idol to the present place of the temple.

Toonderi Rana o gwaru powala rakhi ji o,
Gwaru powala menugeri dhara ji o,
Lacha chari menugeri dhara ji o,
Menugeri dhara o nyiji muruti asayji o,

Nyiji muruti o sata muruta niguti ji o,
Gwalu powala e ghare jogu heri ji o,
Roje roje o menungeri dhare ji o,
Roje roje yada bisoori ji o,
Churure seenge o pathura bahnai ji o,
Bouti seibi o churu duhne geyi ji o,
Shari churi o latana mari ji o,
Shankheri dooguru e pathura lagi ji o,
Bouti seibini gali mowali deeti ji o,
Toonderi Rana e shadi kari ani ji o,
Bolo powala e kya e kama keeti ji o,
Jiya mere saiba e meri arja suno ji o,
Menugeri dhare o nyiji muruti asay ji o,
Nyiji muruti o sata muruta niguti ji o,
Sata muruta khela khelande ji o,
Toonderi Rana e hukuma deeti ji o,
Gachho powala e pithi chaki ani ji o,
Kano muruta e pithi chaki ani si o,
Powala putura e menugeri dhara ji o,
Kana - - — — — - — ayai
Toonderi Rana e jala koonde aye ji o
Shawe koro e shawe dandwata kiti ji o,
Prabhu Krishuna e kune muluke aye ji o,
Bouti seibini jalakoonde ayi ji o,
Shawe koro e shawe dandwata kiti ji o,
Toonderi Rana e vihara basayi ji o,
Toonderi Rana e toondeh Pori chhari ji o,
Loko o duniya e Toondeh Pori heri ji o,
Loko duniya e ghiwe sanjoti bati ji o,
Shawe koro e shawe dandawata kiti ji o,
Prabhu Krishuna e kouna muluke aye ji o,
Bayari padhura e dhumuku chherayi ji o,

SONG ABOUT GURU GHANTAL MONASTERY

Guru Ghantal monastery is one of the oldest monasteries of the valley which is respected by all villagers. This is an historical event regarding the establishment of this monastery which had its origin in Ladakh but was shifted to Keylong by Thakurs.

Tandi Ghusheri sala na gwayi o,
Upuru Ghantaleri dosha na bhooyi o,
Triji lambura e dhoona chhona kiti o,
Negi Hri Chanda poochhune lagi o,
Triji lambura e kiji kame aya o,
Sonu lambura e jawaba diti o,
Raghu lambura e jawaba diti o,
Khoku lambura e jawaba diti o,
Tandi Ghusheri sala na gwayi o,
Upuru Ghantale ri dosha na bhooyi o,
Negi Hari Chanda kalaboota likhi o,
Ayo kalaboota Tambelleri utari o,
Jori manu e Ladakheri bheji o,
Jori manu e Ladakha pounchi o,
Jori manu e Tambelleri ghare o,
Badi guru e Kolonga pounchi o,
Kolongeri Thakura jalakoonde aye o,
Chocho saibini jalakoonde ayi o,
Lok o duniya e jalakoonde ayi o,
Badi guru e ranguteri phere o,
Badi guru e Gundhuleri kothi o,
Gundhuleri Thakura e jalakoonde aye o,
Chocho saibini jalakoonde ayi o,
Gundhuleri Thakura e badi adura rakhi o,
Badi guru e upuru Ghantala geyi o,
Jori manu e Ghushe jogu bheji o,
Trakhuna Raghu shadi kari ani o,

Trakhuna Suguru shadi kari ani o,
Upuru Ghantala nawe lagi bani o,
Upuru Ghantala banguleri nwhare o,
Tandi Ghusheri salana pheri o,

Chapter - VIII
MUSICAL ANALYSIS

To a layman the term "Tribal Music" generally connotes one of two things. The first is a concept of music geographically restricted to a particular tribe as its own special brand, and the second is a picture of music as a special type passed from generation to generation. To some extent both concepts have some truth in them. But the answer is not so simple. Music is not something that one can view in its totality in space as one could see a painting, a building or a sculpture and then describe it accurately. Music is an ephemeral art which has to be felt in. Its very transcendence nature makes it difficult for easy comprehension, specially when it is separated from ritual or function and is then categorised as art music. However, a good working definition of tribal music could be," music which has originated through the ages in conformity with tribal tradition and function.

Tribal music, then is functional and as such it must necessarily need to be studied as an aspect of social behaviour. It is really a multi-science discipline in which the social and anthropological aspects are no less important than the musicological. It is more a field of the ethno-musicology than that of the musicologist or musician. To collect and play back and react to tape recordings of such music is an easy process but it gets one nowhere, however, quaint or interesting the music might be, to understand, it requires a careful study of not only its form and content but also its origin, history and social context. We must try to understand why it has developed its own peculiar form and what the words, rhythms, melodies and gestures mean. In other words we have to treat music as a behaviour trait and study it in the social context.

Tribal music in general has certain common features in India. Dr. Sudhibhushan Bhattacharya, a pioneer in the field of Indian ethno-musicology has mentioned some of them. Tribal music may be termed uncultivated music and the tribes in India may generally be grouped into three categories - the primitive tribes, semi-tribes and semi-castes. Starting with a music predominantly di -, tri-, or tetratonic with single melody line and a symmetrical rhythm, we find gradual enlargement to tetra or pentatonic scales, multi-linear melodic structure and simple 3 or 4 beat rhythms. Further, from functional and ritualistic aspects, the music becomes non-functional and entertaining. Tribal music is very ancient preceding Vedic music. Scholars are now more or less agreed that a well developed system of music might have existed in India before the advent of Vedic period. Such music was predominantly pentatonic, *Matanga* Muni in his *Brihaddeshi* (about 400 A.D.) points out the influence of the tribes on classical Indian music. He refers to tribes such as *Savaras, Pulindas, Kambhojas, Vangas, Kiratas* and others. In fact some of the modes (parental scale of *Ragas*) are named after tribes such as Saka, Abhiri, Gurjari and so on. *Matanga* Muni named eleven of them. Later writers named others such as the *Savari, Koda* and *Gondkiri*. The Vedic people had a powerful language but not well developed system of music. That came later borrowing freely from the rich heritage of the tribals in India.

Alain Danielou, the well known musicologist has made certain observations in this respect, like the forms in language, musical modes are permanent marks of tradition to which a people belong.

The people of Lahaul are quite ignorant about the classical music yet they sing every type of song. The songs though cannot be categorized yet for the sake of study they have been grouped as social songs, songs related to fairs and festivals, historical songs, political songs and romantic songs. These songs are usually accompanied with dances and various instruments.

It has been observed that only five notes are used in most of the songs. The combination of *sa, re, ma, pa, ni* notes is prominent in the tunes of these songs.

In the tunes where *Gandhar* and *Dhaivat* swars have not been used, the next note *Nishad* is used in its flat form i.e *Komal Nishad*.

Every type of song has its own peculiarity for example, the wedding songs are full of joy and happiness whereas the songs sung at the time of the departure of the bride are very pathetic and heart rendering. They are full of the feelings of separation.

Different types of emotions have been expressed through these songs. The historical or political songs are serious in nature. They describe many stories that are sung during fairs and festivals and are very joyous and full of the feelings of happiness.

It is the speciality that some songs are sung in the mornings only and some in the evenings only. In the renderings of these songs, the folk singers use many technicalities of classical music. But they are quite ignorant of the fact and these qualities are expressed spontaneously and without any knowledge or effort. These are their natural expositions, particularly the traditional "Ghure" songs are the best examples of these.

The historical songs are also sung on the occasion of specific festivals or ceremonies. The songs having political themes are sung in the praise of country, state or place of historical importance along with the incidents of political changes. Mainly these songs are accompanied by dance and musical instruments, particularly the flute and drum. These days the use of western drum has become popular instead of the traditional drum.

The love songs having romantic themes are the mirrors of the social set-up of Lahaul. These songs are more popular among the young people. They sing these songs accompanied by dances. Due to their nature of fast tempo they are suited to the dances.

Apart from these songs, the folk singers compose many songs according to the need of occasion.

The most traditional and ancient style of folk songs is the "Ghure" which are the true pictures of the social, political, historical or economical situations and other developments. These songs are sung in chorus. First, the leader of the group sings a line of the song and then other participants repeat the same and the song is completed in the same fashion. In contrast to this, other songs are sung in an altogether a different style. First of all the tune of the song is played on the flute and then is followed by the singers and dancers. The singers sing the song while the dancers dance on the beat of the tune and song. "*Ghure*" are usually not accompanied by any instrument. The whole of the Ghure is sung only in one tune and in slow rhythm. Other songs are of fast tempo. Usually the songs are set to three, four, six, seven or eight beats of *Tala*. They are sung in "*Mandra Saptak*" or "*Madhya Saptak*". The range of the notes used are limited to one octave only and they are sung in slow tempo.

The use of classical *Ragas* is quite evident in some of the songs but the Lahauli folk singers are ignorant about the use of *Ragas*.

Due to the geographic diversities, Lahaul remained cut off from the main Himachal Pradesh and the country. Moreover availability of less educational facility is also one of the major factor that the people of this area are backward in their social and economic conditions. Due to lesser means of communications, the music of Lahaul is still in its original form. It needs to be preserved and protected by documenting since there is danger of the intermixing of the culture of the neighbouring areas and it may lose its originality.

The songs are set in simple *Talas* having six or eight beats. In some cases the Tala having seven or fourteen beats are also used. The instrumentalists who accompany the songs or dances on various instruments are ignorant of what they are playing yet, they play some very intrinsic technical feats of various phrases on these instruments.

The eight beats *Tala* can be equated to the Kehrawa Tala, the seven beats with the *Chanchar*, six beata with the *Dadra* or the *Khemta* etc. But style of playing, the pauses and division of beats is quite different from the classical *Talas*.

To the accompaniment of Lahauli folk music only three types of instruments are used viz membranophonic, aerophonic and ideophonic. The chordophonic instruments are not seen in Lahaul. The most popular instrument is the flute. All types of songs are accompanied by flute. Even a small boy who grazes the sheep can play on flute. With little effort anyone can play the sweet and melodious tunes on the flute.

Among the membranophonic instruments different types of *Dhols* are used. *Dholaki* is very popular. It provides rhythm to every type of song and dance. In addition to the *Dhol* and *Dholaki*, *Paun* is an essential instrument which adds melody to the atmosphere. Its serene and deep sound fills the atmosphere with music.

The *Thali* is the most used instrument among the ideophonic instruments. On the rhythm of the *Thali* accompanied with *Dholaki* and flute the dances are performed. The rhythm provided on these three instruments create a very enchanting atmosphere which reflects the culture and tradition of Lahaul.

GLOSSARY

A

Aktori	Pancake
Along	Golden earrings for women
Arakfsara	A special type of local wine
Ashadh	Fourth month of Indian Calendar
Ashtadhatu	Mixture of eight metals, used for making idols
Avalokita	Lord Shiva
Avalokiteshwar	Lord Shiva
Ayurvedic	Indian System of Medicines

B

Bada Phull	Gold nose pin for ladies
Bagh	Leopard
Bajantri	Musicians, especially instrument players
Baisakhi	Seasonal festival of Lahaul, usually celebrated in the spring season
Bansuri	Flute
Beta	A community of singers, nomads
Bhairon	Security guards of Lord Shiva

Bhatta	A priest
Bhod	Tribe of Spiti valley
Bhot	A Tibetan tribe
Bhoti	Language of Tibetans
Biyahonaraga	Wedding songs of Lahaul
Brajeswari Devi	Synonym name of Goddess Durga
Bugjal	A musical instrument
Bunan	A local language of Bhaga Valley

C

Chabu	Gown worn by Bodh women
Chaitra	First month of Indian Calendar
Chaitrory	Festival connected with agricultural activities
Chapati	A loaf
Chela	A disciple
Choga	Long skirt worn by men and women, like a robe
Chham	A type of dance
Chhang	A local brewed intoxicating drink
Chhaj and Ghuma	Parts of Nagara
Chhodpa	A dance will pentomine performance
Chhota Phulli	Small nose pin for ladies

D

Dadra	A type of Tala of 6 beats
Dangkri	Hair pin made of silver
Dariraga	Songs sung during Jatra
Darshan	Glimpse
Dhareksa	Type of songs, also known as Ghure
Dhatura	A drug plant
Dholak	Two headed percussion instrument
Dhoop	Incence used for prayer
Diva	A girl
Diwali	A festival of lights
Doltog	A special vessel for preparing tea
Dongza	Festival of Lahaul
Doo-sattus	Poridge of barley
Dunkertsa	Ornament used to tie hairs of ladies

F

Fakir	A saint

G

Ganthur	A kind of soup
Ghee	Butter oil
Ghure	Traditional historical songs
Gompa	Buddhist temple
Gotsi/Gochi	A festival on the birth of a son

Grahni	A worshipping process
Griphi	A group dance of Lahaul
Guithah	Gold or Silver ring
Gutha	A songs sung at the time of procession of Lord Shiva
Gura/Guru	A priest

H

Halag/Khogal	New Year Festival of Lahaul
Halda/Halra	Festival of Lahaul
Hessis	A community of singers, nomad

J

Jagra	Worship performed during whole of night
Jatra	Holy journey
Jogi	A saint
Jos	Chief

K

Koba	Wind instrument made of metal, usually brass
Kani	Fried rice
Kanwar or Kamrup	Assam of today
Kapur	Metal used for preparing Poshel
Kawari	A preparation of barley flour used in offerings

Kehrawa	A Tala of 8 beats
Kirkitsi	Silver clips for tieing hairs for ladies
Kothi	A village, cluster of houses
Krishna	A God connected with Mahabharata who was closely associated with Pandavas
Kullavi	Belong to Kullu, language or a person
Kundre	Idol made of brass
Kunh	New Year Festival of Lahaul
Kuth	A medicinal plant of commerce
Kyix-kyirts	Saucer shaped ornament worn over the plaits by women.

L

Lahaula	Inhabitants of Lahaul
Lakshmana	Brother of Lord Rama
Lama	Tibetan priest
Lanka	Srilanka of today
Losar	A famous festival of Lahaul
Lowad	A loaf like preparation
Lugadi/Lugari	A local brewed intoxicating drink

M

Madhya-Saptak	Middle Octave
Magh	Eleventh month of Indian Calendar
Mahabharata	Holy scripture of Hindus connected with Lord Krishna, Kauravas and Pandawas

Mahishasur-mardini	Goddess Durga
Manchat	A local language of the Chadra Bhaga Valley
Mand	Name of Indian classical raga
Matang Muni	Author of Brihaddeshi-a treatise of Indian Music.
Munda	A tribe and language of Bengal and Central India
Murki	Ear-rings for men
Mutig Kanti	Head ornament for ladies

N

Nagara	A pair of drums
Nang	Silver bangles for ladies
Nishad	Seventh note of Indian musical scale
Nyishan	Pair of drums

P

Padma-Sambhawa	Missionary from Kashmir
Pandava	Sons of Pandu who visited Lahaul and other hilly areas during the end
Pandit	A priest
Pangawal	Pangi area of Chamba
Parvati	Wife of Lord Shiva
Paun	A typical percussion instrument of Lahaul somewhat similar to Dholak

Phab	A local herb
Phagli	A festival of Lahual New Year festival
Phans	Silver ornaments for the head of ladies
Phaphada	Yeast
Phempra	A vegetable soup
Pholunu	Silver chain worn by ladies
Poshel	Pair of round balls worn over the either side of forehead of ladies
Prakarma	Round of the temple
Punya	A good deed.
Pyajama	A tight wear for legs, generally for men.

R

Raga	Indian melody
Rahu	The lunar node
Raja	A king
Ram	Hero of Ramayana, usually regarded as God
Ramayana	Holy scripture of Hindus connected with Lord Rama
Rani	Queen
Ransingha	Wind instrument of C shape, made of silver or bronze
Ravana	King of Lanka
Rigole	Nagara like instrument
Rishi	Saint

S

Sadhu	A saint
Samadhi	Meditation
Sangam	Junction of rivers
Shaini	A dance of Lahaul which is traditional and in slow tempo
Shamsham	Collection of chains, ornament
Shaneel	A type of thick silken velvety cloth mostly used for making garments for ladies
Shank	Conch, musical instrument
Shashur	A major fair of Lahaul. Also known as Chhesu
Shiva	One of the most worshipped Lord in Lahaul
Shiva lingam	Idol of Lord Shiva
Sita	Wife of Lord Rama
Sugili or Surgini	Songs of eulogy
Swangla	Tribe belonging to Swangla area of Lahaul

T

Tala	Rhythm
Tambariya	A religious festival and also a dance
Tarka	Clip like ornament for ladies
Tuk Kanti	A necklace for ladies
Thakur	A brave/warrior community
Thali	A plate of bronze used as musical instrument

Thanka	Paintings of Buddhist style in monasteries
Thungpa	A dish prepared from meat
Tinan	A local language of the Chandra Valley
Tishkori	Thick cake like loaf
Trutshati	Rice preparation with vegetables

U

| Utanalohri | Lahauli New Year starts on this day |

V

Vaishakh	Second month of Indian calendar
Vajravrahi	Another name of Goddess Durga
Vasishtha	Guru (teacher) of Lord Rama

W

| Wazir | Minister of king |

Y

Yashoda	Mother of Lord Krishna
Yore	Festival of spring season in Lahaul
Yutod	A round cap worn by ladies

Z

| Zari | Golden embroidered cloth |

INDEX